POTHOLES
&
PIGSTIES

POTHOLES & PIGSTIES

A Prodigal's Journey Home

# C.E. Lenamon

### Edited by Kathy D. Weber

PIPPIN
PUBLISHING

Waco, Texas

## In Appreciation

To my faithful dinner gang – Joy Endsley, Marta Latham and Barbara Pederson. Thank you for praying me through the rough spots. A very special thanks to Kathy Weber for her encouragement, keen insights and whose editorial contributions made this book possible. Love and kisses to my daughter Jayne whose call on a rainy Saturday filled my despondent heart with sunshine. A heartfelt thanks to all who opened their hearts and shared their prodigal stories so that I would know I was not alone. A special thanks to Cassandra and Parrish for sharing themselves and Grace so unselfishly when I needed them the most.

## Journey Thanksgiving

In deep appreciation to those who helped me understand God's grace: Stan Owen, Carole Taylor, Dudley, Betsy, T.D. and Sarah Hall, Chuck Swindoll and Max Lucado. Thanks to my friend and teacher, Stan Latham who through his kind persistence nudged me forth in my journey.

And most of all a loving embrace to my husband Ronnie who was there for me.

# Dedication

To Jayne, Parrish and Mom
for your unconditional love on the journey.
And to my darling Grace.

Edited by Kathy D. Weber
Cover design by Steve Fryer

**POTHOLES & PIGSTIES**
© 1997 by C.E. Lenamon
Published by Pippin Publishing
P.O. Box 8052
Waco, Texas 76714-8052

Printed in the United States of America

**Library of Congress Catalog Card Number: 97-92182**
ISBN 0-9658964-0-4

# Table of Contents

# Foreword

"Christians cannot live in sin, that's all there is to it. You cannot love Jesus and choose to live a lifestyle of sin." I was not surprised at this statement from my friend, Don, as much as I was saddened. For at one time in my life, I too believed this with all my heart and soul. Fighting back the flood of emotions, I said simply, "Oh yes they can, Don. I know, because I did."

My dear friend Don, so pure and childlike in His faith, had a heart of gold. I knew he would never say this to hurt me. He didn't know my past, he only knew the person I had become over the past few years. He saw a confident, successful woman who had an honest heart for God.

Don's comment nagged at me for months following our conversation. How prevalent was this belief? It didn't take much research to discover that many people held to this doctrine. And the doctrine is pretty cut and dried. If you have accepted Jesus as your Savior, you do not want to sin. If you do sin and are sorry, you are forgiven and things are fine. The flip side of the doctrine is not so fine. If after accepting Jesus as your Savior, you sin big time and end up living a lifestyle of sin, then you were never really a Christian to start with.

I knew from my own tale of woe that this doctrine does not play out in human drama. And my story was not an isolated only-time-in-all-of-history experience. I knew others.

I knew Christian women who'd had abortions and lived in guilt-ridden misery for years afterwards. I knew a missionary pastor who'd left his wife and children for a sweet young thing. Today he's an alcoholic. I knew a single mom who in her loneliness had fallen for the lies of a married ex-pastor and chosen him over her faith and family. I could go on. They are out there. They are called prodigals. People who have at one time in their lives had an intimate experience with God . . . then something went wrong.

Each prodigal story is different and yet the same. Prodigals have sought and found their own way apart from God. But it isn't quite the life they expected. They may have what they were looking for, but it isn't making them happy – nor can they find peace. I know because I've been there. Through most of my life I've wrestled with God for control, wanting things my own way. Consequently, not one step on my spiritual journey has come easy. While others naturally found their way, I bucked and rebelled. I was determined to make God fit into the box I had drawn for Him.

He, of course, had other plans. He allowed me to rant and rave, and make life decisions without consulting him. He let me fall on my face and dust myself off, only to fall on my face again. He watched while I paid the consequences of my life decisions. Silently, patiently, he waited, until the day only he knew would come. The day his prodigal daughter would make her journey home.

Much of my life I'd rather forget, but my Father brought me through it, and he did it for a purpose. He has given me compassion for people who crave forgiveness but think they have gone too far and lived too much. People who knew God intimately years ago, but because of calamities in their lives or choices they made, turned away and can't find their way back.

If you are one of these people, take heart. Don't let the guilties knock you down again. God knows you've been down that road too long. There is a way to find what you've lost.

# INTRODUCTION

# WHAT IN THE WORLD
# IS A PRODIGAL?

There are several great stories in the Bible that answer this question. To give you a modern day account, I engaged some artistic license and rewrote a chapter from the Gospel of Luke.

Imagine, if you will, Jesus coming to earth today. No longer sandal-shod but scuffing dust in thrice-soled cowboy boots. Hair still long. Eyes still piercing. The consummate rebel with a cause. The pavement is his desert, the slums his garden. Hookers, con-men and the homeless follow his call as well-tailored suits evade his knowing glance. His church is a body of believers, not a crystal building. Peaceful yet daring, he shuns the religious hobnobbers, scattering their bingo tables in a fit of temper. The God-man is beloved and despised. A companion to AIDS victims and an enemy of the self-righteous, religious crowds.

"Hey, you! Yeah, you with the boots. Why weren't you at church last night? You're supposed to be the son of God.

"Yeah, we know what *you* were doing. You've been running with Freddy the Finger. Don't you know that guy's bad news?

"Somebody saw you eating down at Momma Rosa's with Teddi DeLane and Mimi Reseau. Man, do you know what those chicks *do* for a living? What kind of a religious person are you?"

The God-man sighs, turns to the religious crowds and stares into their empty eyes. Patiently, he begins to tell them a story. "My father's world is different than your world. It's like a certain rich man who had two sons . . .

# PART 1

# THE STORY

# 1

# LEAVING HOME

"Jimmy, will you *please* sign these checks before you leave?" asked Carolyn hurrying to catch up with him. "I have to send them out with the contracts before three."

"What a slave driver you are!"

Carolyn could not help smiling and winking at him as she asked "What do I tell Bruce if he calls?"

"Oh, just pull one off the list," Jim grinned as he scribbled his signature on the clipboarded checks Carolyn held. "Used a doctor's appointment lately?"

"That one's so used up, he's going to start wondering if you have a terminal disease," she laughed.

"Dentist?"

"You could have had all your teeth pulled and shiny new caps by now!"

"Okay, then. Tell you what: *This* time inform Mr. President that his brother has left for the day because his secretary couldn't come up with a good reason for him to stay." With that, the elevator shut, and Carolyn's expression of mock protest faded into a weary smile. Just another day of covering for Jim Barber.

Deciding to walk the twelve blocks home, Jim rehearsed the speech he was to give his father that evening at dinner. He would offer his stock to his father, who had first right of refusal, and then ask for his inheritance. *After all, it's mine and why should I wait? It's better to have the money now, while I'm young and can enjoy it . . .*

"Well, look who finally showed up . . . Mr. Fit. Enjoying the athletic club more and more these days I suppose," murmured Bruce before Jim could say anything.

"And hello to you, brother," Jim answered good naturedly.

"Why hello, Jim," greeted Byron Barber with a bear hug to his younger son. "How have you been? We keep missing each other at the office. You must be busy. How's that Sheridan deal coming? You get the contracts sent off today?"

"Sure, dad. Deal's sealed and delivered. No sweat." Thanks to Carolyn, Jim thought.

"Greta has dinner ready, let's go on in and you can tell me how you set up the contract while we eat." After Byron said a simple yet thoughtful prayer, dinner conversation focused on investment options with Byron and his eldest son volleying opinions and prospectus evaluations back and forth across the table.

"Jim, what do you think? Will Scripter's R&D turn up anything new?" asked Byron. "Jim? Is anything wrong?"

"Sorry, Dad," Jim paused. "Look, I really need to talk with you. Go ahead and finish your dinner, I'll wait for you in the study"

Bruce took the cue and retorted, "No problem, little brother, I'll have dessert later. I've got to get back to the office. *Somebody's* got to pick up the load."

Byron had hoped that time would settle the differences between the two brothers but if anything it seemed that time made things worse. For Bruce, the seething was covered by a thin layer of civility. Tonight even the civility seemed stretched to a wear-through point. If their mother had lived, things would have been different, Byron reflected. A home needs a woman. Jane had been a wonderful mediator when the boys were small – always fair and just – listening to their squabbles and sorting things out. Whatever stood between them now seemed destined to continue.

By the time Byron closed the door to his study, Jim was sitting behind his father's desk, feet propped up as if he owned the room. Deciding not to notice, Byron walked over to the red leather wing back chair facing the desk and eased himself in with a grace reserved for distinguished statesmen and dignified CEOs.

"What is it, son? Is there a problem?"

"Not really a problem, Dad, but a decision. And it isn't a decision I made overnight. Please, if you will, listen to what I have to say, before you interrupt." Even as he said it, Jim knew the request was completely unnecessary. His father was the last of the true gentlemen, bringing wisdom, patience and keen insight into every situation. Jim envied his father's seemingly natural discipline, although not enough to try to emulate his ways. Maybe when I'm older, thought Jim upon admiring his father's reserve. Realizing the two men were silently weighing each other, Jim pushed his chair back bringing his elbows onto the desk. Planting his feet squarely in front of him, he braced for the confrontation.

"Dad, I'll come right to the point. I've decided to get out of the company and I'd like to sell my stock." Jim waited but his father sat quietly. Nervously, Jim played with the antique silver paper weight setting on the desk before him.

"I know this may seem sudden, but I can assure you it's not. I'm not cut out for the business world. It's torture for me coming in everyday and faking it. I'm not sure what I want," Jim lied, "but working 14 hours a day like Bruce does, is not it."

Byron sat quietly as his son nervously ran his hand through thick brown hair, reminiscent of his mother's. *Oh, Jane. How I've spoiled this son of ours*, Byron thought. *He has your hair and your eyes and it was so easy to love him and give him the desires of his heart.* A sad smile crossed his lips which Jim took as a sign of encouragement.

Gaining confidence, Jim rose from the desk chair and went over to his father. "Dad, there's more. I'd like my inheritance also." Byron's face froze. He couldn't believe his ears.

*His inheritance? Why on earth? What would he do with all that money? It's insane.*

"Dad?" Jim said uneasily. "Didn't you tell Bruce and I that all you had was ours? I remember hearing you say that. Did you or did you not tell us that it belonged to us? Am I asking for something that isn't rightfully mine? You know I've worked hard . . . I'm due!"

Byron, trying to regain his composure, rose from the chair and walked over to the fireplace. Putting both hands on the mantel, he kept his back to his son until he could trust his voice. Once in control, Byron asked slowly, "Jim, what do you plan to do with the money?"

"Find my own way, Dad. I'm tired of being Byron Barber's son. Don't you get it? I've lived in your shadow all my life. I want to see what I can do on my own. Dad, I respect your values because they work for you, but they're not my values. It's time for me to be my own person. I want my freedom and independence. I don't want to have to answer to my father every day of my freakin' life." Pausing, Jim realized he had gone too far, but was committed to playing this out. "I want my money. Is it mine or not?"

Hurt and outraged that his son would use his generosity as a weapon against him, Byron sadly walked to his desk, pulled out his checkbook and signed away his son.

"Well, it shouldn't surprise either one of us Dad," Bruce commented the next morning, thinking about the considerable shares of stock that eventually would fall to him. "After all, Jim obviously didn't have his heart in the business. He spent more time at the club than in his office. I don't care what excuses his secretary came up with, they were all lame."

"Bruce, not now," pleaded a weary Byron. "I should think you'd be as concerned about your brother as I am."

"Dad, he's a big boy. He can take care of himself and he certainly has the capital to do just about anything he wants." Seeing that his father was clearly distraught, Bruce changed directions. "Look Dad, you still have me, and you know you can count on me to do whatever it takes."

Byron smiled sadly and put his arms around his eldest child, "Yes son, I know I can count on you."

As seasons dissolved into seasons and years faded one into another, Jim no longer walked in his father's shadow. Completely cut off from his family, he was lost in a world that neither loved nor cared for its victims. The day after he left his father's house, Jim had packed up his clothes and had flown first-class to Paris, in search of his dream.

"Darlin, I wush my ole man could see me now," Jim slurred, moving awkwardly and tipping over the bar stool with a resounding crash.

"I think you've had enough, Mr. Barber, and I ain't your darlin," said Thomas, the burly American Jim had befriended on the street that evening. "It's time for you to go home."

"Nah, justa little one, okay?" begged Jim. "An anotha roun for the house."

Tom knew that Jim wouldn't remember him the next morning, so he half-carried, half-dragged Jim out to the curb and into a waiting cab. After giving the chauffeur fifty francs and Jim's address found in his wallet, Tom walked back into the club and wondered what would possess a man like Jim Barber to waste his life.

Even the most casual observer could see that Jim's life spiraled in the wrong direction. Seemingly hell-bent and determined to live as much life as he could in the shortest period of time, Jim suffered his mornings in bed with a serious hangover and a faceless woman. His afternoons were vague recollections, spent in the experience of a new drug. Jim Barber's flat was a gathering place with crowds drifting in and out – blurred visions of fleshy parasites in search of prey. Occasionally Jim dried out long enough to become restless with his life and invent a new diversion; a chartered jet to Monte Carlo or a yacht from Cannes, filled with newly acquired friends who hung on for a free ride. His indulgences and obsessions drained his resources more quickly than he even knew.

To Jim, it seemed to happen abruptly. "But monsieur, I have funds. Check my accounts again, S'il vous plait." Jim said to the bank teller. The middle aged gentlemen allowed Jim's request and moved back from his teller cage to the computer. As he repeated the steps involved in checking Jim's account balance, he hoped for this young man's sake that he had made an error the first time.

"Non, monsieur, it is the same. As I told you before, we cannot cash your check. There are no funds."

"This is preposterous, let me talk to your supervisor," Jim said indignantly.

"One moment please," the teller answered.

Only after being threatened with a call to the police did Jim agree to leave the directeur's austere office. Stunned, he stood on the curb of the busy boulevard outside the Parisian bank, not fully comprehending his plight. *How could this happen?* he wondered as he sat on the dirty sidewalk in his silk Armani suit.

"Mr. Barber, what are you saying?" asked Catherine Belieu, not believing her ears. The rich, charming American was making excuses instead of paying his rent. In the ten years she had leased her flat, she had heard them all before and had learned not to be sympathetic. After all she was a businesswoman. "You have no money for your rent, but your lease is not over."

"I know, I know. If you'll just give me a few days, I'll come up with it. It's a banking error, I'm sure I can straighten it out, but I'll need time."

"Mr. Barber, you have until five o'clock tomorrow evening, at which time I will change the locks and you will, as you Americans say, be history. Adieu." Jim stared at the phone in his hand. He hadn't expected her to be so tough, after all she was a woman and he was Jim Barber. *C'est la vie, tomorrow something will turn up, after all I'm not completely broke, I still have my Rolex, Mercedes and ring.*

Unconsciously, he slid the ring back and forth on his finger remembering the sunny afternoon of his eighteenth birthday. Walking through the gardens that framed the west end of their vast estate, both father and son felt the importance of the moment. Contemplative and solemn, Byron Barber cleared his throat and broke the silence. "Son, this is an important day in your life. You will have new responsibilities and privileges as a man. As you are allowed to make choices, think through them carefully and make them wisely. There are sure consequences to every action. Some will be good and some will be bad, depending upon the wisdom of your decisions. By example and teaching, I have tried to instill in you a belief in God and a respect for yourself and others. These values, if adhered to will serve you well and will enable you to draw strength to overcome adverse situations and temptations that will come your way."

Byron turned, his handsome face reflecting the dignity required for such an occasion, and presented a purple velvet box to his son. Silently, Jim opened the box and slipped the gold ring with the Barber seal fashioned in sapphire and rubies on the ring finger of his right hand. Barber men for centuries had proudly worn the seal, given to them on the day they entered manhood. Jim knew that this ring would be a part of his being, never to be removed, even to the grave. "Thank you father . . . I will make you proud of me," was the only answer suitable for the moment.

"You must be confused, monsieur," the American said. "I paid thirty-five thousand U.S. for that watch, and the ring is certainly worth more than you're offering me for the both."

"That is my final offer," replied the jeweler. "Do as you must, but you won't receive a franc more in Paris, I assure you." Defeated after bargaining with every reputable jeweler in the city, Jim stuffed the money into his suit pocket and dashed for the airport.

Landing in Monte Carlo, Jim followed the familiar route to the casino. "Good evening, Mr. Barber, it's nice to see you again. Are you alone?"

"Yes Girard, but with a little luck . . . " Jim let the sentence trail off as he winked to the doorman. That evening proved no different than others; Jim had more luck with the ladies than with the dice. Losing all but a few francs, enough to pay his companion, Jim consoled himself with too much liquor, too many pills and his love of the night.

*Thank heaven for round-trip tickets*, Jim thought as he left Orly Airport and headed back to his flat. His plan to win

27

back his fortune had failed. *I'm not flat broke . . . I still have my Mercedes.* Happy-go-lucky Jim felt his first twinge of despair as he drove through the crowded streets of the city he now considered home. If Catherine was as good as her word, he only had four hours left in his furnished apartment. And somehow he thought she might just be as cold-hearted as she sounded on the phone yesterday.

He had never appreciated the decor of his rented flat, but now that he was about to lose it, he noticed how extraordinarily fine the furnishings were. True, the damask drapes were a little worn but in their time the fabric had been rich and discreetly opulent. While the wood plank floors felt cold to his feet, they added warmth to the eye. Several times he had planned to sit in the chintz-covered chaise by the window to read the morning paper and to drink his coffee. His mornings were actually afternoons on most days and the news seemed old before he got to it, so he never bothered.

As Jim gathered his bags, his thoughts went to another time when he left all that was familiar. He allowed himself just a moment of melancholy as he wondered about his dad and Bruce. But when he left his apartment, he immediately shut the door, leaving locked inside the twinge of guilt that tugged at his soul.

# 2

# THE LONG ROAD HOME

No matter how long Jim stayed away, Byron Barber would never become accustomed to seeing only two place settings at the dinner table. Even though his younger son had only occasionally come for dinner, three place settings had always graced the table, just in case. After the stormy night of Jim's departure, Byron's longtime housekeeper Amanda thoughtfully told Greta to remove the setting in hopes of eliminating further pain to the kind man who had been more like a father than an employer to her. "Mr. Barber, will you be retiring soon?" asked the solicitous maid.

"No Amanda, I believe I'll take my coffee into my study and read awhile, but you go on. I won't need anything further this evening."

"Very well sir," Amanda said trying to read his eyes. Even though he had kept up a courageous front, Amanda knew how much her employer had suffered over the antics of his outrageously selfish son. She would never understand how Jim could sever ties so brutally with his father, hurting him the way he did. She would like to give him a piece of her mind and would in fact, if they knew where he was. Not a word from him in all these years, imagine the self-centeredness – it was truly beyond her. *He needs a good lesson and I hope he's getting it,* she sighed as she entered her room on the third story of the elegant Victorian style home.

Jim's lesson came like a shock of cold water.

"Bonjour Jacque. It's Jim. Jim Barber. Ami, I need a favor. It seems my bank is holding my funds until a check clears from the States. Shouldn't take but a day or two . . . in the meantime, I'm a little strapped. Jacque? Jacque? Are you there?"

"Suzette, darling. It's Jimmy. Listen doll, I need a place to hole-up for a few days. Oh, they're doing some remodeling in my flat – nothing serious . . . Sure, I understand. With company and all, you're a little crowded. Sure angel, catch you later."

Jim's plans were dashed with each phone call made from his table at Chez Rouge. The rich American whose money had seemed endless was an amusing diversion for a time, but that time abruptly ended. Money gone, credit cards maxed out, Jim's future appeared bleak until he remembered an off-hand comment made by the manager of the Chez Rouge, Monsieur Arquet. In desperation, Jim tried to piece together the conversation. At the time he had laughed, thinking how absurd the suggestion was but now it might be his chance. "Yes, it could work," he thought brightening. "Pierre, a drink, s'il vous plait," Jim called to the garçon. "Put it on my tab. Oh and Pierre, is Monsieur Arquet in his office?"

"Oui, monsieur, would you like to speak with him?"

"Oui," answered Jim already feeling better. As soon as Jim saw the manager coming toward him, he knew he should cut the bull and go straight to the chase. This might be his only chance.

"Bonjour, Mr. Barber, I'm rather surprised to see you, I heard you were having some difficulties," Monsieur Arquet opened the conversation and took the seat across from his customer.

"Word travels fast among friends," Jim said dolefully.

"Ah, you shouldn't be surprised, you know, you traveled with a fast group. I tried to tell you when you first moved to Paris. Do you remember?" asked Arquet.

"Yes, I do. In fact, it was that very conversation I was thinking about tonight. Look, I'm going to level with you," Jim's voice took on a confidential tone as he learned forward in his chair and locked eyes with the man whom he hoped was his last remaining friend in this fickle city. "I've blown all my money. I'm broke, washed up. I lost my flat today, sold my jewelry, and all I have left is the Mercedes. I figure it's worth about forty-thousand U.S. That's it, that's all I've got. I have no place to live and I won't go home. Even if I wanted to, my family's through with me."

"So you come to me. Pour-quoi?" asked Arquet. "I am not a wealthy man. I cannot give you money."

"I'm not asking for money." Jim took a long drag from his cigarette. "I need a place to stay – to get myself back together . . . I can't stay in the city." The sentence hung in the air.

"Ah, the farm. You remembered our talk about the farm," Arquet chuckled. "You laughed at me when I mentioned it to you before, and all I was suggesting was that you come for a visit. You had no interest in pigs and goats, as I recall, even though the air is so fresh with lilacs and heather, and the setting is more charming than on any postcard. So now, you are interested?"

"Yes, I'm interested," Jim answered, nearly hating this man for making him beg. "I don't expect to live there for free, I can help out. Didn't you say you could use a hand? Surely, with you staying in the city, your brother could use a hand?"

With that Arquet lost his reserve and laughed until his eyes watered. Taken aback, Jim asked what on earth was so amusing. "You, working on a farm?" Arquet barely got the words out in between guffaws.

"I'll have you know I'm quite experienced with farm work," said Jim, readjusting the french cuffs on his hand-tailored shirt. "My family owns ten thousand acres upstate. As a child, I spent most of my summers there."

Solemnized by Barber's apparent hurt feelings, Arquet still could not imagine those soft manicured hands baling hay and repairing fences. But, he did need help, and if Jim was willing to work for food and shelter, he might be a God-send. Arquet studied Jim. Behind that aristocratic exterior was a frightened and desperate young man. Finally, he shrugged his shoulders. "All right, Monsieur Barber, I'll give you a chance. But there will be no second chances, comprendez-vous?"

Jim's face broke out into a relieved smile as he put forward his hand for a gentleman's shake. "Comprends, Monsieur. You won't be sorry, I promise you. Oh, and one more favor, can I sleep in your office tonight? Tomorrow, I will leave for the farm."

"Yes, I suppose it will do no harm for you to stay here one night, but you must tell no one. It is against house rules," advised Arquet. "I will come early tomorrow morning to unlock the door. And you must not sample the wares. We keep a very tight inventory, any missing and I could lose my job."

"Do not worry, mon ami, you have saved my life."

Jim felt extremely proud the next morning that he had kept his end of the bargain. Without one more drop to drink, he had gone to bed early, and had awakened full of anticipation for his new adventure. He was about to turn over a new leaf, get his life back together, make something of himself. Even if it meant shoveling pig slop for a few months.

Selling his car was easy, but finding a pickup that matched the ride of his Mercedes was not. He finally settled on a new Ford with an extended cab, fully loaded. Buying jeans, work shirts, boots and a heavy jacket, on a whim, he took his city clothes to a charity and dropped them off, hoping the recipient of his generous offer would appreciate the imported silks and fine Pima cottons. Satisfied that he had what his new life demanded, he unfolded a map, laid it on the seat beside him and started off for the Arquet farm.

Mile after mile of lush countryside confirmed that Jim had made the right decision. Here nobody knew him. The embarrassment of losing his money would not be an issue. He could reinvent Jim Barber any way he wanted, as long as Arquet would keep his mouth shut. The fresh air and friendly waves from passersby brought back memories from his childhood and served to remind him of what he had thrown away – and for what? *For fun that's what. And to be my own person. And that's exactly what I have achieved.*

At dusk, Jim pulled into the one-lane dirt road that led to the cottage where he would be staying. Glad he was making this trip with enough daylight to see the white gate, Jim made his final turn.

"I am sorry, Monsier Jim, I told you last week why we cannot eat breakfast at 10 am." Arquet's brother, Robert, said with as much patience as he could muster. "Farm life is different than city life, oui?"

"Oui," Jim said flatly. Learning the ways of farm life from Robert proved more than Jim had bargained for. Each evening he massaged oil onto his swollen and cut hands before he crawled into bed, only to drag himself out of bed at dawn the next day.

Robert Arquet wondered at his brother's ill-conceived plan to help this soft and obviously spoiled young man. *He puts more energy into getting dressed for his one day off than in feeding the pigs the other six days.*

On Saturday, Jim's day off, and on any day he could sneak away, he claimed his table at the tavern that sat on the edge of town. He found pleasure with two sisters who worked for their father in the tavern, and with locals who passed away their day betting on anything from arm wrestling to crows flying. Once again, he was in his element, playing fast and loose with the money left over after he bought his truck. But it wasn't long before the locals, the sisters and the French countryside bored him and he was ready to move on.

Arquet was not surprised when on his fifth visit to the farm since Jim's arrival, his new hand had saved him the embarrassment of the long overdue talk they both knew was inevitable. During the night, Jim had packed his bags and was gone without a thank you or note of good-bye. Nor was he surprised when he heard some months later that Jim had gotten himself into some trouble with a woman in a farming community some miles away.

"I warned him, I pleaded with him. What was I to do? I told him that no good would come from his life. He is a young man headed for destruction," wrote Robert Arquet to his brother.

It took exactly one year for Jim to live out Robert Arquet's prophetic words. Money gone, he gambled his truck and lost. Living in an abandoned barn and eating less than Robert Arquet fed his pigs, Jim begged for money as he walked along the country roads. Occasionally, a compassionate traveler stopped to give him a few coins for food, which Jim hoarded until he had enough for a bottle of cheap wine.

The end of his begging came the day three local hoodlums decided to teach the vagrant a lesson. Beating Jim unmercifully, they left him on the side of the road to die. He lay in a pool of his own blood until a widowed farm woman stumbled across his body. Frightened, she ran back to her house in search of help. Her two strong sons carried Jim's limp body across the field and into a tiny room off the barn.

The boys bathed and dressed Jim's wounds while the mother stood vigil over her charge. Unable to pay for the services of a local doctor, the good woman put her trust in a higher authority. Praying for Jim's recovery, she sat quietly by his bed day and night nursing his wounds and singing softly the hymns she had loved since childhood.

Jim's healing came slowly as he faded in and out of consciousness. "Mother?" he tried to say once, but it came out so garbled, the woman had no idea what he was trying to communicate.

"Shh, shh, child. Sleep is what you need."

Eventually, Jim's body healed. The kindness of the woman had an impact on Jim that went deeper than his wounds, but he didn't know how to repay her. It left him feeling worthless and more alone than he had ever felt in his life.

"You are still very weak and have nowhere to go. Don't leave us, Monsier!" pleaded Jim's gentle host. Deeply touched by her concern, Jim could not answer. Instead, he continued to gather his meager possessions. She knew further words were useless. But there was something more she could do for this poor, dear man. She pulled out a small square of cotton tied with yarn and placed it in his hand.

Jim took the gift, hugged the woman who had saved his life and left the farmhouse. With nowhere to go and no hope for the future, he wandered for days eating berries and greens and sleeping in abandoned shelters.

Exhausted, hungry and despondent he yearned to fade into the countryside, weightless as a spirit. His body heavy, he trudged through a field late on a cloudy afternoon. The fall winds blew his long tangled hair into his eyes, nearly blinding him as he made his way up the grassy knoll. Stumbling over rocks, catching himself before he fell, he prodded onward, as if compelled to see what lay just beyond the rise. What he found was a valley of sheep grazing lazily. As he approached, they neither acknowledged his presence or cared that he existed, and the peacefulness of the scene soothed Jim Barber's senses.

Coming to a chestnut tree, he collapsed to the ground, resting his back against the trunk. Disoriented and not sure how long he had been there, the sound of the man's singing brought him out of his slumber.

Seemingly oblivious to the intruder, the shepherd walked toward his flock carrying a lone lamb across his shoulders. "My sheep hear my voice and know me, I call my sheep by name," sang the shepherd in perfect French and with a clear tenor voice.

The scene was so other-worldly that at first Jim thought he was dreaming. He stayed very still so as not to disrupt the tranquillity of the moment.

"There you are wanderer, " the shepherd said to the lamb as he tenderly removed him from his shoulders and set him down on the ground to graze. "Maybe next time you'll think twice about wandering away from me. Surely you were a bit concerned that I would not find you, leaving you to wander the earth in search of substance."

As the shepherd began to count the remaining sheep to make sure all one-hundred were accounted for, his eyes found Jim huddled against the chestnut trunk. Silently, the shepherd walked the short distance to the tree. As Jim looked up to the tall man standing only a few feet from him, he was startled to see the kindest, clearest eyes he had ever beheld. He could not remove his gaze, nor could he speak, he could only stare. The shepherd lifted the strap of a leather canteen over his head and silently offered water to the stranger. Jim eagerly accepted the gift and drank hungrily from the vessel allowing the liquid to run down his chin onto his filthy clothes. Jim sensed that the water had been drawn from an unusually deep well; its purity was beyond definition. It satiated his thirst and hunger immediately, unlike anything he had ever experienced.

"Who are you?" Jim's whispered tone breaking the silence sounded strange to his ears.

"I am the shepherd," was the reply. "I am sorry that I was not here when you arrived. One of my sheep wandered away and I have spent the day looking for him."

"But you have so many," Jim observed. "You left all the other sheep, just to search for one?"

The shepherd smiled and explained simply, "Sheep when they stray cannot find their way back. The one that wandered was lost. He needed me. Come, it's getting late and you need warm clothing and food." Not waiting for Jim to answer, the shepherd began to round up his flock. Jim struggled to his feet and followed the stranger through the valley to his humble, but inviting cottage. There he found a simple but nourishing meal, a warm bath, fresh clothes and shelter for the night.

The shepherd was gone the next afternoon when Jim finally awoke. How long had it been since Jim slept in a warm bed? To him it seemed like centuries. Jim knew he could never repay this stranger who took him in and asked nothing in return. As Jim was dressing, he remembered that in his tired stupor the night before he had dropped one of the ten coins given to him by the kindly farm woman.

He looked around the bed but could not see it. He crawled on the floor beginning to panic. He looked in corners and pulled out the dresser from the wall to no avail. He could not give up, this was all the money he had in the world.

Tears streaming down his face, he caught his reflection in the mirror and gasped in horror. He walked over to the dresser and stared at his own sunken eyes not recognizing the once handsome face. "Oh God, what have I become?" cried Jim putting his head in his hands as he began to sob. "Oh God, help me. Please help me. Save me from myself." Jim sank to the floor once again and held himself in a ball, arms hugging his knees as sobs racked his body.

How long he sat crying, he didn't know, but when he finally was able to stop, he felt strangely refreshed and more lucid than he had been for a very long time. He let go of his legs and dropped his hands to the floor, his fingers coming in contact with an object. He stared in disbelief. His lost coin. How important it seemed to him now; the coin that was lost was found. Much like the shepherd's one little sheep. Even though he had others, it was important that none should be lost.

A truth came perfectly clear to him in that moment: He was lost but could be found. He had a family, a home. His father's servants lived far better than he did – they had shelter, food, warm clothing. He would never expect his father to take him back as a son, but could he refuse to take him back as a servant? And if not a servant, a low-paid employee in the company? Surely anything is better than starving to death in the middle of a foreign country. His pride gone, he was willing to beg.

It took Jim time to talk his way onto a freighter crossing the Atlantic, but eventually he was hired as a deck hand. Fighting nausea throughout the trip, he was miserable, but determined. The weeks at sea gave him time to prepare the speech he would give to his father. He rehearsed it until he knew it by heart. *Father, I know that I have done a terrible thing. I've said and done things to you that hurt you greatly. I not only sinned against you, but I sinned against God. I don't expect or deserve your forgiveness. I'm not asking you to accept me back as your son, but if you could find it in your heart to allow me to work for you as a gardener or in your mail room at the company, I promise not to let you down again. I'll stay out of your way and work hard. All I need is food and a place to live.*

The day Jim had been longing for finally arrived. Unable to move, he stood across the street gazing up at the tall glass building with The Barber Company logo in white letters across the front. Cold, drizzling rain made him shiver, but still he was unable to move across the street. Losing his nerve, he was about to leave for shelter when a familiar looking face came into his view. He saw his father bounding across the street.

"Jim? Son, is that you?" cried Byron Barber. Reaching Jim, Byron put his hands on Jim's shoulders and drew him close. Tears streaming down his cheeks and his arm protectively around Jim's shoulders, Byron led his frail son across the street into the lobby of his building.

"Dad, I can't go upstairs. Could we talk here?"

Byron answered with a smile, "Oh, son, anywhere you want."

"Dad," began Jim, "I am so sorry. I have done a terrible thing. I've sinned against you and God."

"Jim, Jim," his father interrupted, "that's all in the past. You're home and that's all that matters. Oh, son, you'll never know how much I missed you. I have been standing at my window each day you have been away, longing to see you, and today, there you were. I couldn't believe my eyes. I ran to the elevator, hoping when I got down here it wouldn't be my imagination, but that my son, my dear son, was finally home."

Overcome with emotion, Jim and his father openly wept and held each other for several moments while passersby stared with bewildered expressions.

Driving home, Jim became apprehensive about seeing Bruce and even the house servants. "Don't worry son. Everyone will be so glad to see you. Please, let's put the past where it belongs and enjoy the present," Byron entreated Jim. But Jim wasn't so sure.

"Amanda, Greta . . . everyone!" Byron Barber called out, "See who is home. Come quickly!"

"What on earth is all the commotion about, I haven't heard Mr. Barber sound like that since . . . oh, my stars, Greta, it couldn't be . . . " Amanda stopped dead in her tracks upon seeing Jim Barber, or someone who looked like a much thinner, older version of Byron's younger son. "Jim?" she asked, "Is that you?"

"Oh Amanda, Greta, you'll never know how good you both look. I'm so glad to be home," Jim grabbed them both forgetting how he must smell.

"My lands, you need a bath. I'll go draw it for you. I still remember just the way you like it," replied Amanda backing away from his arms.

"Not on your life . . . I'm a big boy now. You don't have to wait on me," the old charm coming back in his smile but with a new depth of integrity and humility. With that Jim bounded up the steps to his old room on the second floor. At the landing, he called back, "But I could sure use something to eat. Would you mind heating up something, Greta? If it's not too much trouble?"

"No trouble, Mr. Barber," Greta said glancing at Amanda, both women amazed at Jim's new found humanity.

When Greta left for the kitchen, Byron Barber motioned Amanda into his study. "We shall have a party." The elder Barber suddenly realized his thought had been spoken. "Yes, a party. A huge banquet, celebrating the return of my son."

"A party, sir?" asked Amanda, not quite sure she understood.

"How long has it been since this house was filled with friends, laughter and dancing?" Byron asked, obviously overjoyed with his idea.

"Not in a very long time, sir. Not since Mrs. Barber . . . " Amanda couldn't finish the sentence, so her employer did.

"That's right. Not since Mrs. Barber passed away. She designed this house to be a home. A home full of love and gaiety. It's time. What better time to celebrate love, family and friends. Amanda, my son is home! We shall have a party. I want the best of everything. Nothing is too good. The best china, the best silver. Music. Yes, music. We'll hire an orchestra. Call Mrs. Jefferson's housekeeper. She'll know who we should have. Oh, and ask her about a caterer . . . I want Greta to enjoy the evening and not spend her time in the kitchen. Call my tailor also. Jim will need a new wardrobe."

Byron's words were coming out so fast, Amanda hastened to the desk for a pen and paper. She wasn't used to planning anything so grand. She would need all the help she could get.

Reading her thoughts, Byron said, "Oh, and call that maid service . . . you'll need help polishing the chandeliers and the silver."

After Jim's much needed bath, he joined his father for warmed-over chicken and dumplings from the evening before. Throughout the meal, he could not keep from yawning, even though he yearned to spend time with his father. Understanding how tired his son must be, Byron urged Jim to rest. "Son, there will be years for catching each other up. Go on upstairs and get some sleep, you look exhausted." Jim hugged his father and gratefully retired to the comfort of his bed, falling asleep immediately.

When Bruce came in that evening, Amanda was talking with Mrs. Jefferson's housekeeper about the plans for the party. Overhearing enough to pique his interest, he went into his father's study to assuage his curiosity. "Hello Father. May I disturb you for a moment?"

"Do come in, Bruce. I have splendid news. I called the office but you were in a meeting, so I decided to wait until you came home," Byron said as he bounded out of his chair to stand before his eldest son. "Your brother is home!" Bruce stood immobile, speechless. "I know how you feel, son, I was overwhelmed with joy, too," said Byron misreading Bruce's silence.

Putting the pieces together, Bruce said, "So we are going to have a party to celebrate the prodigal's return?" asked Bruce, unwilling to believe his father could be so stupid to be taken in by Jim's conniving once again.

"Yes, but more than a party. A celebration banquet with all of our friends, employees and clients. Amanda is finding an orchestra and a caterer. We'll have Simon tailor new suits for Jim. I want it to be the best night this family has ever had, an evening your mother would be proud of."

With the mention of his mother, Bruce lost his

composure. "Mother proud? Oh please, Dad. She would have been horrified at the antics of *your* son. The way he talked to you? God only knows the things he did! I seriously doubt mother would have thought this worthy of a celebration," Bruce said, his caustic tone becoming more belligerent as his anger heated.

"Bruce, that is enough!" Byron said, not believing his son's attitude. "You are talking about your own flesh and blood."

"Dad, that flesh was severed the night Jim walked out on us. I can't believe you would fall for his lies again. Don't you see what he's doing? He's using you," Bruce shouted and stormed out of the room.

Byron slept fitfully that night, not understanding how such joy could turn so sour. To gain one son and lose the other was too much to bare. Bruce will come around once he talks with Jim and sees that he has changed . . . surely, he will, yawned Byron, as he finally succumbed to an early morning sleep.

The two brothers came face to face before dinner the next evening. Jim, feeling somewhat intimidated, waited for his brother's lead. Bruce, with practiced movements and calculated timing appeared genuinely glad to see his brother.

"Well look who it is. My long lost brother!" gushed Bruce.

"Bruce, I am truly glad to be home. I can't tell you how glad." Encouraged, Jim reached to hug Bruce, but instead received an outstretched hand.

"Good evening father," Bruce said stiffly looking over Jim's shoulder.

"Son," answered his father. "Dinner's ready."

The conversation was stilted and uncomfortable for all the members of the Barber family, but matters became unbearable when Bruce noticed Jim's ring was missing. "Say, Jim, you know the tradition. The family ring is never removed. Where is it?" Jim looked stricken, he had forgotten about the ring until that minute.

"It's a long story that I want to tell both of you," Jim stammered. "I just don't know where to begin. I'm so ashamed of myself." Jim's self-effacing attitude took Bruce by such surprise, he was speechless.

Sensing Jim's pain, Byron said, "Son, there will be plenty of time to talk. If you want to tell us, fine, but do it when you are ready."

Regaining his senses, Bruce blurted out, "Dad, I just asked Jim a simple question . . . I don't need a long explanation." Turning to Jim, Bruce asked evenly, "just tell me . . . where is the ring?"

Taking a deep breath, Jim said, "I sold it when I needed money."

Not believing his good fortune, Bruce pounced on his brother, "You sold the family ring and you have the gall to return to this house?"

"Bruce!" his father said sternly. "It's *only* a ring. I will order a new one."

"Oh, that's the limit," raged Bruce, slamming his fist onto the table. "I have stayed by you all these years, slaving away, doing your bidding. And in all these years you have never, not once, given me a party. But your precious son returns from years of doing who knows what and you're buying new suits, hiring caterers, and, now, you're giving him a new ring. Don't you see the injustice of it all?"

As Jim sat silently he understood his brother's anger and yet felt deeply hurt that the reunion he had longed for was not to be. He would give anything to change things, but he could not. There would be consequences for the decisions he had made, just as his father had warned him the day of his eighteenth birthday. Tears stinging his eyes, he looked over to his father who had his head bowed and his hands clasped tightly together at his brow. The room was so quiet, Jim could almost hear himself breathe.

Byron lowered his hands into his lap, lifted his head and said with a controlled but kindly voice, "Bruce, you have always been with me and all that I have is yours. But your brother was lost and now he is back with us. If I had one hundred sons, yet one was lost, I would search to the ends of the earth until that one son was found. That is God's way and that is my way."

# PART II

# HOW DID I END UP
# LIKE THIS?

# ARE YOU A PRODIGAL?

The story of the younger brother has been called the Parable of the Prodigal Son for a very long time. The word "prodigal" is not in the original text of the Bible. I don't know exactly who first thought of the phrase to describe the story, but it stuck.

What does "prodigal" mean? According to Webster, a prodigal can be anyone who is exceedingly and recklessly wasteful. For the purpose of this book, I am defining a prodigal as anyone who at one time in his or her life accepted Jesus Christ as Savior, but has exceedingly and recklessly wasted the *means* of God: the supernatural power God releases in the lives of his obedient children.

> The power to look up at a sunset and
> whisper, I love you, Daddy . . .
>
> The power to spend countless hours with
> him and enjoy his company . . .
>
> The power to look into the mirror and see
> his greatness in who you are . . .
>
> The power to turn your back on anything
> you know he wouldn't like . . .

The power to forgive and be forgiven . . .

The power to have peace in your soul.

God's means are the love and power he knows his children need to live abundantly free. But many are not free. Are you?

1 a. Do you have an intimate relationship with Jesus?
   *or*
   b. Are you too racked with guilt to enjoy his companionship?

2 a. Do you pray and know that God hears you?
   *or*
   b. Have you quit praying?

3 a. Is your life wide open to the Lord's scrutiny?
   *or*
   b. Do you shudder at the thought of God's intrusion into the darker moments of your life?

4 a. Do you hate sin?
   *or*
   b. Do you wallow in sin, enjoying its pleasures?

5 a. Are you able to overcome temptation?
   *or*
   b. Do you fall into temptation's trap?

6 a.  Can you forgive yourself, as well as others?
    *or*
  b.  Do you hold resentments and grudges?

7 a.  Do you have inner peace and joy?
    *or*
  b.  Do you need noise and activity to drown out your cries for help?


If your "b" answers far outweigh your "a" answers, don't be discouraged. At least you're honest. That's a good beginning. In the following chapters you will learn that you are not stumbling through life alone. Believe me, there are many Christians sliding and tripping on the same rocky path. You'll discover that Christians have been doing this for centuries. And you'll discover that God has a plan for you. A way for you to stop. Turn around. And walk in a new direction.

Many like myself can relate to Jim Barber's misadventure. And there are thousands, perhaps tens of thousands, sitting in church pews all over the world today who, if they were to search their hearts, would see themselves as the second prodigal in the story — the older brother. Continuing to lead upstanding and moral lives, they are hurting and many times rotting from the decay of resentment and unforgiveness. They judge without love, shielding their own insecurities in a cloak of self-righteousness.

Some of you reading this book will recognize immediately that you are a prodigal. Others might discover it through reading this book. There are certainly degrees of prodigal living, as evidenced by the story of the younger and older brother. You can hurl yourself into a life without God, or you can quietly and methodically withdraw from God's presence. No matter which form of rebellion you chose, the end result is not the life Jesus promised to all who abide in him.

Before you tune me out, remember that I too, was a prodigal. I understand how easily you can go from singing "I'd rather have Jesus" to slurring "Ninety-Nine Bottles of Beer on the Wall." I am not some religious book writer. I am just a woman who has made some really crummy decisions in her life. For awhile, I pondered the possibilities of crawling in a hole when Jesus returned so I would not have to face him. For a long time I believed I was beyond hope, and at times I didn't even care. In my twenties and early thirties, my conscience feelers were so singed from playing with fire, I did not know right from wrong anymore. But I could not deny God's tug inside my soul. I knew that I was a born-again believer and I knew God was not pleased with me. I struggled against him for years. I was a self-willed, spoiled brat who wanted my own way . . . and God wanted his. While I won countless battles, he triumphantly won the war.

Tune in. Listen closely.

From the pages of this book, you'll feel the tremors of the battlefield. My futile strategies of combat. His tactical plan for victory.

# 3

# THE JOURNEY BEGINS

You have probably heard that a Christian's life on earth is a journey. It starts when you believe in Christ and it ends when you go to heaven. Sounded easy enough when we were saved, didn't it? Most of us started our journey skipping along the yellow brick road singing a "Happy, happy, joy, joy" song. I did. Then I came to a fork in the road.

*Which way now?* Hesitantly I slowed my step and edged to the left. OOPS! The Wrong Way sign popped up before my eyes. Sensitive to the warning, I retraced my steps. On the right track again, I began to feel more confident. Skip, skip, "happy, happy," skip, skip, "joy, joy."

*Oh no, a detour! Hmmm . . . I'm supposed to keep my eyes on the map, but down that road is something that looks mighty intriguing. Just a few steps . . . who will know? What will it hurt? Think I'll try it awhile!*

Skip, skip . . . stumble, trip. *What was that?* Skip, skip, stumble, trip. Skip, skip . . . crash.

I found myself in a pothole. At this point, I could

have reached up, grabbed Jesus' hand and followed him back to the road he had laid out for my life. I knew I was on the wrong road because it was a much wider road and it had stumbling blocks and dangerous potholes along the way. I had been given specific instructions to keep my eyes on the journey map. Instead, I focused on the scenery around me, took my eyes off the map, stumbled and fell. Into potholes, ditches, canyons. Did I admit I was wrong? No, not me. Instead, I chose to explore the crash sight. I sunk deeper and deeper and deeper. It got darker and darker and darker. Pretty soon, my eyes became accustomed to the dark and I could no longer see the light that illuminated the map for my journey. I blindly but willingly sunk into my chosen hovel.

The worst part was I loved my pit. Although some days I hated it. I made New Year's resolutions that lasted a short time then lashed out at myself for being weak. I had been away from God for so long and had done so much, I couldn't imagine returning. How would I find the right road? What would I say to God? Would he even want to talk to me? I visualized a fearsome, vengeful God who was waiting to zap me again. (Sound familiar?) I couldn't honestly say to God that I would leave my off-the-track life behind. I had tried so many times and failed. So I stayed put. Immobilized.

When terrible things happened in my life I secretly felt that God was punishing me. Part of my brain told me that I deserved it, while the other part railed against God. Sometimes life's hurts provided further justification for staying away from him. But other times, I nervously prayed that God still heard me and would help me.

Because I have been there, I know that many of you – deep down inside – want to climb out of your pit, but don't know how. Some of you will not admit it, not even to yourselves. But you feel God tugging at you, as I once did. And you know that the life you are living is not the best life you can lead.

The one thing every prodigal needs to hear is that there is a way out. There is no chasm too deep or too wide for God's rescue team. No addiction too strong. Whether you are sitting in jail right now or in a church pew, God meets you just where you are. When Jesus came to earth, he did not hang out with saints, he searched out the sinners. His friends were ordinary men and women . . . tax collectors and prostitutes included. He would rather hear Freddy the Finger crying out to him for mercy, than a church leader congratulating himself for being a righteous man.

*Oh sure*, you might be thinking, *that sounds good, but you don't know what I have done!* No, but I know what *I* have done. And believe me, if God could forgive me and bring me to the place I am today, there is immeasurable hope for us all. And to prove it, I am going to give you some gory details from my life as well as from others. And I am going to show you how to crawl out of the quagmire . . . one foot in front of the other, one step at a time.

I ask only one thing from you.
        Close your eyes for ten seconds.
        Open your heart.
        And say to God,
            "Please, help me to understand."


Now, let's explore the real story in the Gospel of

Luke and see what Jesus had to say. But first, a little background:

"Dishonest tax collectors and other notorious sinners often came to listen to Jesus' sermons; but this caused complaints from the Jewish religious leaders and the experts on Jewish law because he was associating with such despicable people – even eating with them!"

*So Jesus used this illustration:*

*"If you had a hundred sheep and one of them strayed away and was lost in the wilderness wouldn't you leave the ninety-nine others to go and search for the lost one until you found it? And then you would joyfully carry it home on your shoulders. When you arrived you would call together your friends and neighbors to rejoice with you because your lost sheep was found.*

*Well, in the same way heaven will be happier over one lost sinner who returns to God than over ninety-nine others who haven't strayed away!*

*Or take another illustration:*

*"A woman has ten valuable silver coins and loses one. Won't she light a lamp and look in every corner of the house and sweep every nook and cranny until she finds it? And then won't she call in her friends and neighbors to rejoice with her? In the same way there is joy in the presence of the angels of God when one sinner repents."*

*To further illustrate the point, he told them this story:*

"A man had two sons. When the younger told his father, 'I want my share of your estate now, instead of waiting until you die!' his father agreed to divide his wealth between his sons.

"A few days later this younger son packed all his belongings and took a trip to a distant land, and there wasted all his money on parties and prostitutes. About the time his money was gone a great famine swept over the land and he began to starve. He persuaded a local farmer to hire him to feed his pigs. The boy became so hungry that even the pods he was feeding the swine looked good to him. And no one gave him anything.

"When he finally came to his senses, he said to himself, 'At home even the hired men have food enough and to spare, and here I am, dying of hunger! I will go home to my father and say, "Father, I have sinned against both heaven and you, and am no longer worthy of being called your son. Please take me on as a hired man."'

"So he returned home to his father. And while he was still a long distance away, his father saw him coming, and was filled with loving pity and ran and embraced him and kissed him.

"His son said to him, 'Father, I have sinned against heaven and you, and am not worthy of being called your son.'

"But his father said to the slaves, 'Quick! Bring the finest robe in the house and put it on him. And a jeweled ring for his finger; and shoes! And kill the calf we have in the fattening pen. We must celebrate with a feast, for this son of mine was dead and has returned to life. He was lost and is found.' So the party began.

"Meanwhile, the older son was in the fields working; when he returned home, he heard dance music coming from the house, and he asked one of the servants what was going on.

"'Your brother is back,' he was told, 'and your father has killed the calf we were fattening and has prepared a great feast to celebrate his coming home again unharmed.'

"The older brother was angry and wouldn't go in. His father came out and begged him, but he replied, 'All these years I've worked hard for you and never once refused to do a single thing you told me to; and in all that time you never gave me even one young goat for a feast with my friends. Yet when this son of yours comes back after spending your money on prostitutes, you celebrate by killing the finest calf we have on the place.'

"'Look, dear son,' his father said to him, 'you and I are very close, and everything I have is yours. But it is right to celebrate. For he is your brother; and he was dead and has come back to life! He was lost and is found.'"[1]

[1] Luke 15: 1-32, LB

# 4

# DETOUR AHEAD!

When you read the story of the younger brother, didn't you think his penchant for the seedy side of life was his downfall? I did too, at first. But when I searched deeper into the characteristics that alienated him from his father, I gleaned something more. I saw a young man puffed-up with pride, demanding control of his own life. In his immaturity, he could not comprehend that his father's ways were best for him. So, he took control. And when he did, he careened *out* of control.

**Detour: The Boulevard of Control**
Control: To exercise authority over; direct; command

Many modern-day Christians have turned into prodigals by snatching the reins from God and riding herd over their own life. Some did not trust God enough to direct their lives. Others gave into a temptation too tantalizing to resist. Some really head-strong Christians, like myself, are guilty on both counts. Knowing the road I should have traveled, I paused at the detour intersection a second too long. Seeing something I couldn't resist, I took control and made a wrong turn.

Taking control from God leads Christians to the darkened, dangerous byway, the Boulevard of Control. We prodigals know this wide, deceptively alluring boulevard only too well. It is the mother of all breeding grounds. We sprayed cute little Gizmo with water and saw the killer gremlins pop out. And the longer we played, the more gremlins we stumbled over. Some of us stumbled over lust and sunk into immorality. Many tripped over greed and somersaulted into idolatry. Others staggered over anger and plummeted into unforgiveness or even murder. Along the way, some lost their trust and slumped into fear. While others doubted God and crashed into the canyon of the faithless. And the longer we prodigals swaggered down the Boulevard of Control, the more arrogant and haughty we became. Like a lasso from Satan, pride bound us up and brought many of us toppling down.

It's easy to gallop off the right path in hot pursuit of control. We live in a society that worships control. A society singing, "I Did it My Way." A society intoning, "I am the master of my fate, I am the captain of my soul."[1] Control is a safe house for most of us. Trust is hard, because we have been let down too many times by those we have trusted. Eventually, we trust few people to do the job like we can, or to keep a secret, or to love us as we need to be loved.

And when we need an answer to one of life's everyday questions, we need it now. We demand instant answers with our instant coffee. And God is so invisible and quiet at times. For God to be in control, we need to hear him. We want a sign from heaven and if we don't get it, sometimes we will make it up. My favorites are the people who open their Bible, close their eyes and stick their finger on a passage. They believe that where their finger lands is God's answer for the moment. Unless, of course, the answer is not what they wanted and they try again until God gets it right. But who am I to judge? I did not wait for God either. I took charge, just like the younger son. And all the killer gremlins had a field day.

If you think back on your first wrong turn, you'll probably discover that you were guided by the wheel of control. You may have wanted something or someone you knew you should not have. You did something you should not do. Like I did, you decided you knew better than God. Wanting it badly, you did not trust him to come up with a better answer. You defiantly demanded your way, took control and went for it. And years later, you are still paying the price.

And what God wanted all along was to personally escort you down the road he had paved for your life . . . a well-lit road with a journey map for directions, and well-worn footprints in which you could walk.

But we are not the first, nor probably the last who chose the wrong road. Exercising authority over God is not new. It's as old as the ancient world.

Just look at King David. Anyone who listened to his third-grade Sunday School teacher tell Bible stories, heard the one of David's sling-shot victory over the giant Goliath. From that propitious event, David went on to be the King of Israel. He was a mighty warrior, favored and loved by God. In fact, David's name in Hebrew means beloved, and he was described by God as a man after His own heart. David's name is mentioned over one thousand times in the Old and New Testaments of the Bible – more than any other name!

David had everything going for him. He ruled over thousands, loved and married beautiful women, fathered many children and lived in a palace. Then one day while walking on his terrace, he *happened* to glance into his neighbor's bedroom window and saw his neighbor's wife, Bathsheba, naked. At that moment, you better believe David knew what he *should* do. But instead, he had an affair. The events from this point on went from bad to worse. When Bathsheba discovered she was pregnant, David took control. He contrived a plan that lead to Bathsheba's husband's death. In essence, David had Uriah killed. So now we have a once-godly king turned adulterer *and* murderer.

About this time, God sent the prophet Nathan to tell David a story.

"David, did you hear the news about the two farmers? One of the guys was rich and had lots of stuff. The other was a poor man and had nothing except a little lamb. He loved it so much he considered that little guy part of his family. The other day the rich man had company for dinner. So, instead of killing one of his own sheep, the rich guy takes the poor farmer's lamb and butchers it. Can you get over it?"

David couldn't believe it! He was so angry, he said, "Any man who is that mean deserves to die!"

Nathan answered David, "Well guess what David, you are the man!"[2]

That got to David. Anguishing over his sins, David repented. When Nathan saw how sorry David was he gave him the good news, "The Lord has taken away your sin. You shall not die."[3] And so God forgave David. But that was not the end. Nathan told David for many years thereafter, he would pay a huge price for his acts of defiance.

And so it happened.

Bathsheba's child died. David's other children turned against him and each other. They murdered, pillaged and raped. Eventually, King David's life settled down and Bathsheba gave birth to another son. His name was Solomon. King Solomon, the wisest man who ever lived.

If you have never spent much time reading the Bible, in particular the Old Testament, you might be shocked to learn that not all the people portrayed in God's Word lived out their lives as saints. In his infinite wisdom, God chose to work out his plan for this world through humans. And then on top of that, he gave us a free will. (Pretty risky on God's part!) Sometimes the people God chose for special projects came through it just fine, but not always. I believe God had a profound purpose for including the stories of those who fell alongside those who performed just as God wanted them to.

The parable of the younger son and the real life story of David show us that God understands how downright human we are. And that our acts of defiance have real consequences. But best of all, they convey the power of a repentant heart and the love of a forgiving God. How different the endings of each story would be without the elements of repentance and forgiveness.

What if the younger son had been too prideful or too racked with guilt to return to his father? What if upon returning home, his father had treated him as the older brother had? Not only would the younger brother have no home or family but his father would have lost a son, and his own life would be destroyed by an unforgiving heart.

What would have happened to David if he hadn't

trusted God for forgiveness? His sins were huge by society's standards. Instead of agonizing over them and repenting, he could have thought "I'm too far gone. I've done too much. God will never forgive me." His guilt-ridden life from that time forward would have been lived out apart from God. How bad would that have been for David? Throughout David's life, he had walked intimately with God. David knew what it was to have a moment by moment relationship with his creator.

In battle, David had been protected.

In his life, David had been blest.

In his heart, David had been loved.

And David knew beyond a shadow of doubt that God, like a loving father, had been the benefactor of all the blessings in his life. For David to lose his relationship with God would have been a fate worse than death.

David had traveled down the Boulevard of Control, stumbling over lust and sliding into its pit of immorality and murder. But he chose not to stay there. He repented and trusted God to forgive him. He swallowed his lumps and paid the price for his mistakes. Rising from the pit, David allowed God to escort him back to the road of life. And from that day forward David knew experientially what it meant to walk hand-in-hand with a merciful God.

I wrote earlier that I could relate to the younger brother's misadventure and long journey home. I can also relate to David. Unfortunately, unlike David, instead of trusting God to forgive me, I chose the guilt-ridden life apart from God for many years.

[1]"Invictus," by William Ernest Henley, 1849-1903
[2]II Samuel 12: 1-7, author's paraphrase
[3]II Samuel 12: 13b, author's paraphrase

# 5

# CONFESSIONS OF A DETOUR JUNKIE

The sixties were turbulent years for many, but somehow I seemed to avoid much of the early political rebellion, not feeling the burning that consumed many of my friends. My mother and grandmother had taught me to trust the government; if we were at war it was for our good. Dinner time discussions always focused on current events – Democrats were good, Republicans were bad – end of discussion. While I did not question the political logic at the time, I began to question my spiritual beliefs. *Who was God? Was there a God?* One evening at the dinner table, I mustered all the courage and wisdom of my sixteen years and boldly announced that I was an agnostic. Silence. Then a huge argument erupted that ended with my stamping off to call a fellow rebel for reinforcement and validation.

In my final semester of high school, after experiencing a two-year period of confusion and doubt, I met Jesus. I've yet to hear anyone explain a conversion experience that would make sense to someone who has not come face to face with the star of mankind's greatest love story. In human terms, it makes no sense. In spiritual terms, it makes sense of everything.

My experience was different from many others, yet had the common theme that binds all born-again experiences together into a single story. I had been a good girl growing up. I went to church every Sunday. I even taught Sunday School with my mother. My grandmother read the Bible faithfully and had taught me right from wrong. I'd always followed the golden rule. Still, something was missing. Though I had believed in God most of my life (except for the short time I tried agnosticism and dabbled in the Eastern philosophies), I simply could not find peace. Nor could I fill the emptiness inside. In my stumbling, bumbling way, I was seeking truth. And the reason for my existence.

It didn't take God long to hook me up with a group of kids that had the answers I had been looking for. I was drawn to them because they seemed to have found peace. They talked of their relationship with God, not of church doctrine. They talked of Jesus as if he were alive . . . and – wonder of wonders – living inside each of them. This last part really spooked me, but for some reason I kept going back for more.

At the time I thought these kids were religious nuts and I certainly would never end up like them. And yet I was inquisitive and wanted to find out why they were so different than all my high school friends. They patiently answered myriad questions as well as they could, concerning beliefs of varying religions, theological differences . . . . Myriad smoke screens for the real doubts I had and I'm sure they knew it.

One night the burden I felt was so heavy and the void inside of me so dark and empty it hurt . . . I knew I had to know. How did you go about having an intimate relationship with the creator of the universe? These people obviously had something I didn't. And what I could see in their lives, I wanted. I wanted to have peace. I wanted to know that I was going to heaven. I asked the questions, and scripture after scripture was presented before me. I laid my doubts out on the table for all to see and the Bible was the only answer given me. Every question I asked had an answer in scripture. I became frustrated. I could read what it said, I just couldn't understand how it related to me.

Growing up, I had spent hours of every Good Friday in church. It wasn't an option — it was a command performance. I remember it was a mournful service that wasted a perfectly good sunny afternoon in a darkened church singing songs of death. But it did give me time to think, and I remember wondering why Jesus had to die. *If he died for the world, what did it mean? What good did it do? What did it accomplish?*

I liked Easter Sunday a lot better. It meant a new dress and a fancy hat. The songs were livelier and everyone was more cheerful. I knew the reason for Easter – "Up from the grave he arose, with a mighty triumph o'er his foes. He arose a victor from the dark domain, and he lives forever with his saints to reign!"[1] I understood in an abstract way that this was good. But for the life of me, I didn't understand how it related to my life today. Except for the addition of a new dress and Easter bonnet now in my closet, by Tuesday when school resumed, the celebration was over and nothing significant had changed.

Years later I was grappling with the same questions.

My intellect balked at such a simple plan of salvation. How could it be so simple and yet so hard to put my arms around? For the life of me, this scene would not play out in my mind. Lying in bed one night, I finally gave up. Fully aware that I just didn't get it, I cried out, *Oh God, please let me see what you have shown others. I want to know you. I want to understand the significance of your Son. I want to go to heaven. I want peace in my soul.*

At that moment, when I knew I could do nothing, he did it all. It was like I had been blinded to the truth and in a second my spiritual blinders were removed. I suddenly saw and understood the mystery of Christ. I began to understand that while the death of Jesus *was* for the world, it was actually a lot more personal. Jesus died for the world, one person at a time. While I was not a murderer or a thief, I had sinned. With God as the standard, I just did not measure up. Jesus died so that I did not have to measure up. He paid the price for me. He died so that I could live. This supreme sacrifice was made by a God who lives in a splendid place, adored by angels. He did not have to come down to earth to intervene in the lives of his creations . . . but he did come. He came because he loved me. And he longed for me to know him – to grow accustomed to his personality and to commune with him intimately.

I came to understand that the empty dark void that most of us feel in our lives is a God-given void. It is there for a purpose. It is there for him. He created us to love him, and when we finally give in, he sends his Spirit to live out his love through us, filling the emptiness with his presence. But too many of us trudge through life trying to fill the void with career, money, booze, sex, drugs, relationships, and even church work. The more we try to fill the chasm, the lonelier and sadder we become. We come to understand that there will never be enough people, and never enough things to satisfy us. Still we keep desperately trying.

The next few years of my life were lived seeking after him and studying his Word. I bubbled over. I had become one of those religious nuts! I told everyone I saw or knew what had happened to me. I wanted all my friends and family to know Jesus in the same way I did. I remember sharing my experience with a lady who said, "Oh honey, I'm saved and I used to be on fire too, but don't worry, you'll get over it, and things will be back to normal for you someday." I was crushed. I thought, *No, not me. I'll never lose this feeling. How could I? It was Utopia — heaven on earth.* I vividly remember thinking, *I'm just one of those people God loves in a special way. My personality will prevent me from ever losing my faith. I guess some people are just cut out for being spiritual and some people aren't.* RED ALERT!

I felt a nudge in my spirit.

I ignored it.

And it wasn't long before these thoughts, brought on by a monumental case of human pride, came back to haunt and mock me.

With the exception of the joyful times with my two children, Jayne and Parrish, my twenties are years I would like to forget. I truly envied those who planned their lives and lived their plans. I admired the women and men who married, raised kids and stuck together through thick and thin. I found consistency in life a virtue to be praised. Yet, even as much as I admired these lifestyles and virtues, I could not seem to live a normal, predictable life. There was a restlessness in me that I could not control.

Much of my six-year marriage felt more like a prison than a relationship. Both my husband and myself were from broken homes, so neither of us had the first clue how a real marriage should work. We were young, selfish and uncompromising. Eventually our me-first attitudes took their toll. I became miserable with my life and disillusioned with my faith. *Why would God allow me to end up with a man like this?* I agonized. *It seems the only time we're not fighting is when we're in church. Is this what a Christian marriage is supposed to be?*

Love gone, faith weak, my life seemed hopeless. I felt trapped, and in my immaturity, I looked outside my marriage for fulfillment. Just as the younger son had demanded control of his life, and just as David had taken authority over his life, I decided I knew better than God did what my life needed. I decided to have an affair.

Immediately the pain of guilt ravaged me. I knew I could not continue living a double life. I was out of fellowship with the One who had given his life for me; yet I couldn't go back to the way things were. And, in all candor, I liked my new sin because it brought a way of escape to my life. After much anguish, I told my husband. He called the elder of the church who came unannounced to our home. It was horrible. I felt wretched. Something he said to me that day lingered to haunt me for years to come. "I know that you accepted Christ as your Savior," he told me, "but you haven't yet made Christ the Lord of your life. I discern you may always have difficulty submitting to his will."

I felt guilty and ashamed about the affair and spent the next week listening to my husband rail against me. Neither of us would accept the responsibility for the troubles in our marriage. Nor were we able to offer solutions to the problems that had pushed me to another man. Deciding that I could not continue the way things were, I drove to a park close to our house and spent several hours thinking, crying and walking around the lake. I don't remember praying. I do remember knowing deep in my soul that the decision I made that day would follow me the rest of my life.

With a confused faith not yet grounded in God's grace, I believed these were my only choices: Stay with my husband, knowing I was forgiven by God; but also knowing I would forever be berated by my husband for my infidelity. Or, I could leave my husband and forever live apart from God. I was acutely conscious of the war being fought for my soul that day. After several hours I said aloud, "If this is Christianity, I don't want it. I can't live out my life being miserable."

Though the Bible talks about grieving the Holy Spirit, I really didn't understand the concept until that minute. A grieving in my soul and spirit pierced the depths of my being. I felt physically sick. Despite this foreboding sign, the choice was made. I decided that day not to trust God with my life. Now in full control, I said good-bye to my husband, good-bye to my church and good-bye to God. What I didn't know as I willfully turned my back on God was that God did not turn his back on me. I may have been finished with God, but God was not finished with me.

---

[1]"Christ Arose," by Robert Lowry.

I hurled myself away from God and began to live the story of the younger brother. Maybe you did too. But what of the older brother? He stayed at home with his dad. He worked hard, followed all the rules and expected others to do the same. And when they did not, he performed the services of judge and jury. With his strong convictions and iron will, he felt no compassion for the weak. He rather gloated in their failures and became incensed when confronted with their successes. He worked hard for his father, but with no real submission, no humility of spirit. He proudly broadcasted his sacrifices. Mercy died in his heart, and resentment grew into bitterness.

He followed all the rules and expected others to do the same. In and of themselves, those are not bad characteristics; without rules our society would be in worse shape than it is today. But when you add the stumbling blocks of intolerance, judgment and lack of compassion, you have a lethal pit of something called legalism. Beware: It is poisonous to souls.

# PART III

# POTHOLES & SNARES

# 6

# THE POISONOUS PIT

**Legalism**
Strict, often too strict and literal, adherence to the law.

While legalism is alive and flourishing in many Christian groups today, its poison infuriated Jesus. One day after putting up with their gibberish for as long as he could, Jesus really let the legalists have it: "You hypocrites! Well did Isaiah prophesy of you. These people say they honor me, but their hearts are far away. Their worship is worthless, for they teach their man-made laws instead of those from God."[1]

Prior to Jesus' time on earth, God gave laws which all Israelites were to follow. The religious leaders took great pride in following the letter of the law. They enjoyed the law so much that they began adding to it. By the time Jesus came, the laws were so convoluted they made no sense – except to those died-in-the-wool legalists.

Jesus was well-acquainted with these leaders, and he witnessed the lives they led. He knew they were puffed-up with pride and intoxicated with self-importance. They shouted their prayers from the roof tops so all could hear and flashed their offerings so all could see. They were back-biters and gossips. They were more concerned about fol-lowing their rules than in listening to the message Jesus came to deliver.

Legalists would rather do the works than live the love. They would rather stand in judgment than stand with their brother in compassion.

As I see it, there are at least two forms of legalism today. The first is salvation by works. Many people, like the religious leaders in Jesus' time, have missed the sig-nificance of Christ's death, burial and resurrection. They think their good works will secure a place for them in heaven.

God sees this as supreme arrogance. These legalists have completely ignored God's word:

"There is no one who does good, not even one."[2]

"All our righteous acts are like filthy rags."[3]

"*All* of us like sheep have gone astray, each of us has turned to his own way."[4]

I don't see any exceptions here, do you? God did not say:

"There are only a few who do good."

"All righteous acts except the ones performed by Sam, Joanie and Bert are like filthy rags."

"Most of us, except the Baptists, are like sheep who have gone astray." No, there are no exceptions. None of us can be righteous on our own, no matter how good we are, no matter how many rules we follow. Christ is our right-eousness. By his grace, we are made righteous – not by his rules.

Those following the second form of legalism understand in principle that they have been saved "not by good works, but through faith,"[5] but they live as if their salvation is contingent upon following the law. Exhibiting little understanding of God's grace, they prefer to be guided by the rules in the book rather than the love that flows out of the book.

I learned firsthand how lethal the second form of legalism can be to a soul. My husband and I attended a church that walked by the letter of the law. As a new Christian, I was like a sponge absorbing everything I could. I didn't know enough to question the doctrines I was being taught.

I hasten to say that there was much good about this church. This was the church that had brought me to the Lord. This was the church my husband's family went to and my in-laws were wonderful, loving people. The members of this church believed they were hearing the Word of God preached accurately. And in part, they were. The trouble was, the don'ts far outweighed the do's; and while the letter of the law was preached, the intent of God's heart was missed.

We hear about the intent of the law in many of our Supreme Court cases. Ten different people can read the same words written on paper and interpret the meaning of the words ten different ways. It is then the responsibility of the court to decide intent. What were the words originally supposed to convey? What should these dynamic words do for society?

While we would like to think that God's Word can only be interpreted one way, it is simply untrue. I do not know if you have spent much time reading commentaries.

These are books written by Bible scholars who explain what each verse in the Bible means. These learned men and women have studied the original Hebrew and Greek languages of the Bible and translate word meanings. I have one commentary that gives several different opinions for nearly every verse. No doubt, this explains the diversity of Christian denominations. Each believes its interpretation is correct. Some denominations are tolerant of other's opinions, while others fight for their right to be the authority.

I firmly believe that the Bible must be studied as a whole. You cannot take one verse here and another verse there and build a doctrine. And you cannot take one law and make it a must-do, while ignoring other laws. God's intent is the most important consideration. Did he give us the Bible to heap condemnation on our heads or to bring us to himself? I am afraid many churches are preaching condemnation in their efforts to scare the hell out of their members. It does not work. We have tried it for generations and now we are seeing the results. Most people do not respond to fear, they respond to the love that meets their needs. (We will discuss more on the life-giving power of the Bible in a later chapter.)

[1]Matthew 15:7-9, LB
[2]Psalms 14:3b, NAS
[3]Isaiah 64:6b, NIV
[4]Isaiah 53:6a, NAS
[5]Ephesians 2:8-9, author's paraphrase

# 7

# CONFESSIONS OF A LAPSED LEGALIST

In the legalistic church my husband and I attended there was a great deal of emphasis placed on the number of times in a week we went to church. We seldom missed. We attended Sunday school, the worship service, the Sunday evening service, the young people's meeting on Wednesday night, the Thursday night prayer service and the couples' club meetings held once a month. When we dropped the Wednesday night young people's meeting, we became leaders of the Friday Club for kids. Obviously, we had little time for each other.

The church did not believe in celebrating worship. Without musical instruments and praise singing, we sat silently with solemn faces and listened to men somberly pray and read from the scriptures. This was being joyful in the Lord.

I was taught that only this church denomination preached the true Word; all others were in error. And the only true Word came straight from the King James translation of the Bible. I was told that all Catholics were doomed to hell, and that Baptists were too liberal for heaven. Charismatics were not worth mentioning.

I bought it all. Who was I to question those who knew the Bible far better than I?

I was told that true believers spoke of the deity as *Lord*. While those who did not know him called him *God*. Therefore, you could instantly judge people by the way they referred to their maker.

I did question the lack of love and trust in the membership, evidenced by the incessant gossip that ran rampant throughout the church. Sometimes it was cloaked in the form of a prayer request for "poor sister Mary." More often than not, it was blatant gossip. "You won't believe what Sue told me . . . or what I saw John do." I had been taught as a child not to "carry tales" because it was hurtful to others, so I knew this destructive behavior could not be pleasing to God.

I began to see other things that did not ring true. As a congregation, we spent so much time *in* the church, busy as a swarm of bees, that we had little time for those *outside* the church. Great importance was placed on "evangelism," but to most that meant inviting a guest to a church meeting or passing out tracts on the street. It did not mean reaching out in love to those who needed Christ's compassion the most.

I was outraged at the bigotry I discovered inside the teachings. I was taught that African-Americans were a condemned race, with a curse from God that would never be lifted. We were to "love" them but advised to stay clear of them. After all, they had a different skin tone than the one tone found within the walls of the church.

The frightening reality is that the people of this church were sincere, fundamentally good people. They loved God with a passion. They honestly believed in what they were teaching . . . and they found it in the Bible. Unfortunately, while following the exactness of the law, they missed the intent of God's heart.

I know that being in this environment for six years radically affected my behavior for the next ten years of my life. In my mid-twenties, when I made the decision to leave my husband and our church, I honestly thought I was doomed. I thought this meant that I had irrevocably turned my back on God. I believed this for a number of reasons. I had been taught that this was the one true Bible-believing church and that what they taught was straight from the mouth of God. I was already defeated because I knew I could not live the rest of my life following all of God's laws to the letter. I was a young woman filled with fun and vitality. I needed some room to enjoy life. I felt too young to take everything so seriously. Secondly, I believed that a divorced woman could not remarry and stay in fellowship with God. Never remarry? Raise my two kids alone for the rest of my life? I could not promise that! Unfortunately, I believed a Christian man should never marry a divorced woman; so later on in my life, I thought unsaved men were my only option. Most importantly, I believed that no matter how sorry I was for my sins God would never forgive me.

Now, let's back-up. Jesus did say all of the things I was taught concerning divorce and remarriage, but let's put it into context. Picture Jesus standing on a grassy hill overlooking the Sea of Galilee. A gently rolling wake licks the shores. Before him sit thousands of men, women and chidren eagerly anticipating the sound of his voice. Most have walked miles to catch a glimpse of this man who claims to be the Messiah. To hear him teach. To feel his love. To touch his garment. As he looks out over the multitudes, his compassion pours forth. He sees past their smiles and into their hearts. And opening his mouth he says, "Blessed are the poor in spirit, for theirs is the kingdom of heaven. Blessed are the gentle, for they shall inherit the earth." [1]

You have probably heard much of these teachings – they are called the Beatitudes. Jesus is revealing his Father's heart, uncovering the qualities in a human that God desires. Then he goes on to give the intent of the law. Yes, it is true that anyone who commits murder is in danger of judgment as the law says. "But I say unto you, that whosoever is angry with his brother without a cause shall be in danger of the judgment." [2] The law says, "You shall not commit adultery; but I say to you, that everyone who looks on a woman to lust for her has committed adultery with her already in his heart. And it was said, whoever sends his wife away, let him give her a certificate of divorce; but I say to you that everyone who divorces his wife, except for the cause of unchasity, makes her commit adultery; and whoever marries a divorced woman commits adultery." [3]

So what do we see here? We see that Jesus' law penetrates to the heart. Whereas these same laws in the Ten Commandments were interpreted as crimes of action. And we see that Jesus made no distinction between the thought and the action.

While the church was correct in teaching that I should not divorce and remarry; they were incorrect in making me believe that it was the greatest sin a person could commit. They did not make the same huge statement to someone who got angry without cause, even though in

God's eyes it was the same as murder. And how many men besides President Jimmy Carter believes that lust is the same as adultery?

Please do not misunderstand, I am not trying to justify my adultery or divorce. In God's eyes it was wrong. He intended for one man to marry one woman, have children and live together as a family unit. This is best for all concerned, especially the children. But I have to be honest. If a battered wife with abused children sought my advice, I could never, ever tell her that God intends her to stay with this man, as I have heard other Christians do. The God I know is not like that.

So what is the intent of God's heart? I believe he wants us to live as Jesus taught. Because what Jesus taught is good for us. However, he knows we will fail in many ways. He knows that baby Christians will have a harder time of it than mature Christians. So he wants us to stay in touch with him, learn from him and grow. When we do fall, he does not want other well-intentioned Christians to beat us down. He wants us to know that while he is not pleased, he understands our frailty. "Just as a father has compassion on his children, so the Lord has compassion on those who fear him. For he himself knows our frame; he is mindful that we are but dust."[4] With our bruised knees and bloody hands, we are not only allowed, but welcomed when we run home to him for healing.

Oh, how I wish I had known that in my twenties.

After my divorce, I decided what was done was done; I had made my bed and now I had to lie in it. I grieved for a moment, then hurled myself into a life without God. I was free at last. No more strict rules for me. One by one, I turned each no into a yes . . . and oh, what a mess I made of the next ten years. On my own, in total control of my life, I careened out of control. I partied and dated, and married and divorced several times. My kids were moved from this home, to that home; met this man, then that man – all because Mom was searching for Mr. Right. You know the one. In every generation he shows up in some TV sitcom. In my generation he was "Father Knows Best." In yours, maybe he was the head of the "Brady Bunch." Today, he is Tim, the Tool Man. All I know is for me, he was the abracadabra man – now you see him, now you don't. I kept trying because I knew every child needs a father, and every mom needs a dad.

While my life spun on a merry-go-round, my spirit remained silent. I made sure my children went to Sunday School . . . just because it was the thing to do. And sometimes my body attended church with my mother, but my heart was not there. Occasionally, when things fell apart and the pain was heavy, I felt really scared, utterly alone and lost. I would lay in my bed curled up in a ball and cry out to God. *Oh, please God. If you can hear me, please, please get me out of this mess I'm in.* From my past, I remembered a verse in the Bible that said, "He lifted me out of the pit of despair, out from the bog and the mire, and set my feet on a hard, firm path and steadied me as I walked along." [5] I clung to that verse and prayed that no matter how bad I was, no matter how many awful choices I had made, God would someday find a way to bring me out of my pit of despair. I prayed that he still loved his little girl. But even when I prayed, I held little hope that he was there.

All these many years later, I wonder how different my life would have been if I had not been exposed to the deadly virus of legalism. If I had not allowed its diseased-

90

ridden condemnation to be heaped on my head, would I have found forgiveness sooner? If I had understood God's love and infinite grace in my twenties, would I have turned my back on God when I needed him the most? If I had understood that there were others who were going through the same things I was going through, would it have mattered? If I had known that there were other churches who taught the Word in love, instead of by the letter of the law, would I have found my way home sooner? I cannot help but imagine the powerful influence a compassionate Christian sister or brother could have had in my life. But I will never know, because I did not even know one existed. Maybe, just maybe, I still would have taken the road I trod. Only God knows.

Even today, there is a philosophy among some Christians that the proper way to handle someone as rebellious as I was is to make sure the sinner knows how bad they are. Make sure they know how much proper Christians hate the sin, but of course, love the sinner – and then stay clear of them. Some Christians seem to have this great fear that if they try to console the errant one they are actually condoning the sin. In my case no one needed to tell me that what I did was wrong. And the prodigals I have talked to admitted the same. They knew they were sinning without having condemnation heaped on their head. They do not have to be told. No matter how many times they try to justify their actions. Deep down inside, they know.

I went into a Christian bookstore recently to see how many published books addressed the topic of Christian restoration. I was heartened to see quite a few; one was even a bestseller. I found several books written for divorced

Christians struggling through forgiveness and self-worth issues. There was one written for Christians whose souls have been critically wounded by members of their church. While leafing through the pages and reading several excerpts, my heart went out to these authors because I knew they had suffered. They were sharing their hearts in hopes that others would be helped through their experiences. But I couldn't help but wonder. Where were these books twenty, thirty years ago? They did not exist, as far as I know. And if they had existed would I have found them?

If there had been Christian bookstores back then, would I have gone in and said to the young man or lady behind the counter, "Excuse me, but I've just committed adultery and I'm going through a divorce. I'm feeling like God will never forgive me and my life is the pits. What would you recommend?" No, I can tell you I wouldn't have. And I am afraid others who need to hear that there is hope are not going to a place where they can find it. They may be like I was – ashamed. Convinced that they will never be forgiven.

[1]Matthew 5:3,5, NAS
[2]Matthew 5:22a, KJ
[3]Matthew 5: 27-28, 31-32, NAS
[4]Psalms 103:13-14, NAS
[5]Psalms 40:2, LB

# 8

# VULTURES WITHIN

**Unforgiveness**
To be resentful, angry; to have the desire to punish.

What makes us feel so totally unforgivable and at the same time so unforgiving of others? Many of us might be too close to the older brother for comfort. He couldn't seem to get past the negatives. Consequently, he harbored unforgiveness, resentment and bitterness in his heart. Walking down the Boulevard of Control, he tripped over his anger and self-righteousness and slid into the pit of unforgiveness.

I recently saw a promo for an upcoming television news show that made forgiveness sound like a new discovery. "Noted psychiatrist, Dr. X has made a scientific breakthrough," blared the announcer's voice, "advising his patients to forgive. Dr. X has discovered that if people can learn to forgive others they will live longer and be happier. This new theory is being tested on ten patients."

But wait! There was more. Mr. Announcer went on to say, "Not everyone agrees, however. Dr. Z says that's rubbish." (footage of Dr. Z) "I believe people should take revenge . . . it's their right to get even. They should *not* forgive. They will be healthier if they get mad and let it all out!"

Aren't we fortunate to have television's deep thoughts to ponder? Shall we forgive or shall we plot an assassination? Will I be happier restoring a friendship or serving time in prison? Of course, if murder is too crass for your senses, you can try other inventive means of revenge. The clerk in your neighborhood video store will point you to any number of movies with ideas offered by Hollywood.

While it does appear quite human to dream of getting even, most of us are too civilized. Instead, we harbor resentment. We tuck the hurt into a closet inside our soul. From time to time we take it out and examine it, turning it over and over so that we can investigate new possibilities for our indignation. Sometimes we treasure it so long we forget why it's there. With the reason gone, do we clean out the closet and throw it away? Not usually. Instead, we hold onto our resentment, if only for justification . . . a reason for our lost friendships and loves.

What does God think about unforgiveness and resentment? In the Bible, Jesus told this story:

> *"The Kingdom of Heaven can be compared to a king who decided to bring his accounts up to date. In the process, one of his debtors was brought in who owed him ten million dollars. He couldn't pay, so the king ordered him sold for the debt, also his wife and children and everything he had.*

*But the man fell down before the king, his face in the dust, and said, 'Oh, sir, be patient with me and I will pay it all.'*

*Then the king was filled with pity for him and released him and forgave his debt.*

*But when the man left the king, he went to a man who owed him two thousand dollars and grabbed him by the throat and demanded instant payment.*

*The man fell down before him and begged him to give him a little time. 'Be patient and I will pay it,' he pled.*

*But the creditor wouldn't wait. He had the man arrested and jailed until the debt would be paid in full.*

*Then the man's friends went to the king and told him what had happened. And the king called before him the man he had forgiven and said, 'You evil-hearted wretch! Here I forgave you all that tremendous debt, just because you asked me to — shouldn't you have mercy on others, just as I had mercy on you?'*

*Then the angry king sent the man to the torture chamber until he had paid every last penny due.*

*So shall my heavenly Father do to you if you refuse to truly forgive your brothers."[1]*

While medical researchers may ponder the benefits

of forgiveness vs. the sweetness of revenge, Jesus has given those who follow him a clear direction. We are to forgive as we have been forgiven. God has told us in the Bible, ". . . for I will forgive their iniquity, and their sin I will remember no more."[2] I have heard people say, "I can forgive him, but I will never forget." God might be the only one who can truly forget. As humans, we may never forget the memory because it is stored in our subconscious. But there is a difference between feeding and caring for the memory and simply recognizing it as a fact of the past. If you can remember the act without feeling pain, then you have truly forgiven. If you purpose to keep the memory alive, you will only harbor resentment. And resentment eats away at your soul.

I have known prodigals who turned away from God because their feelers got stepped on in church. Some were angry with their pastors. Others were offended by a church member. Some were petty offenses while others were more serious. Instead of going to the pastor or a church member to talk it out, they vowed never to enter a church again. I concede that talking it out might not have turned the wrong into right, but even a chance for reconciliation would be worth the effort.

It is a fact of life that not all churches are created equally. Churches are as different as the people who make up the body of Christ. If we were all mature Christians living in peace and unity as Jesus wanted, wouldn't life be grand! But we are not, and a gracious God has chosen to stick with us imperfect humans to run his business on earth. If anyone should be upset and resentful it should be God – not we humans who have messed it up in the first place. Turning your back on God because of a human error is a tragic display of immaturity.

For you who have quit going to church and now snub your nose at fellow Christians, you are hurting not only yourself, but also the body of Christ. In God's infinite wisdom he has given each of us supernatural gifts to be used for the common good of his believers. If you are not exercising your gift within the body, we all are hurting. We are missing the blessing that God knew only you – with your experiences and your personality – could give.

If you earnestly believe that you cannot function in your own church, I urge you to search out one that you feel comfortable and safe in and make that one your home. But please leave your bitterness and resentments at the door. Forgive as you have been forgiven.

I can hear some of you now, "But you don't know what they did to me!" I may not know your story, but I have witnessed enough to make my skin crawl. I know of college boys who were seduced into homosexual acts by a pastor they trusted. I know of a husband whose wife was hustled by his friend, a deacon. I met a minister of a huge church who was charged with an attempt to murder his wife so that he could marry his lover. All of these offenses were committed by once-godly men who after their heinous acts of deception went about their church duties as if nothing had happened. But not for long. Each of these men was caught.

I know for a fact that many members left the church after these incidents of abuse because one of the offenders was my pastor. He confessed to the congregation one Sunday morning that he had been battling homosexuality for years. We sat in stunned silence. Then he resigned. It was an extremely difficult time for our church. Some of us were sorrowful; others were angry. But each of us had some soul-searching to do and some decisions to make. *Should I leave the* church? Should I stay? Should I allow myself to become disillusioned because I was betrayed? Does this mean Christianity is a hoax and I have been deceived? Most of us made the right decision. We stayed, and over the next few years we worked through our grief and rebuilt our trust. But none of us will ever forget the heartbreak we felt for our pastor's lovely wife and young children.

Now here is the twist to the story that presents evidence why we humans are not qualified to judge one another. On the surface, the situation was clear. However, God saw something totally different as he looked into the hearts of my pastor and his wife. We saw a man we had loved and trusted for more than a decade confess to the unthinkable. We felt repulsed, shocked and betrayed. We saw a woman who stood by her man and for whom we felt compassion and sympathy. But what did God see? God saw a broken man who knew how hurtful his sins were. A man who had agonized over his weakness and had cried for help. But try as he might, he could not overcome his sexual addiction. God saw a woman who in her anger and rebellion had kept her own love affair a secret. A bitter woman who was not repentant, but was doing everything she could to get even with her husband – and with God.

The complete story of my pastor and his wife is public knowledge now. Not because we talk of it, but because they share their incredible testimonies as they minister across the country. They tell of their fall from grace, their agonizing struggle to overcome sin, their battle with shame and guilt, and finally, they share their victory. God has graciously healed them and given them a message of hope to share with others who are struggling with strongholds in their lives.

God tells us not to judge, because he is the only true judge. He alone can judge the heart. When we become judge and jury, we are literally saying, "I condemn that person for his offense."

And God says back at us, " . . . judge and you will be judged; condemn and you will be condemned; pardon and you will be pardoned."[3]

And then we say, "But God, that guy's sin is really bad."

God answers, "And why do you look at the speck that is in your brother's eye, but do not notice the log that is in your own eye?"[4]

Despite what they read in the Bible, there are Christians who have chosen to judge the wrong-doer. And faced with that kind of unforgivenesss, many a wrong-doer has left his church family, never to return. If you are one who has stumbled – maybe even crashed – you are probably thinking, "What's the big deal? I can be a Christian without going to church. In fact, I'm a better Christian than those hypocrites who go to my church!" You may be right. It is certainly true that you can be a Christian without going to church, but you will not grow. There is a reason God instructed us "not to forsake the assembling of yourselves together."[5] Each of us needs to be fed.

Jesus, the Great Shepherd, told Peter, "Feed my sheep."[6] While Jesus cares that we have substance for our bodies, he was not telling Peter to go to the grocery store and deliver Lean Cuisines to his children. He was telling Peter to teach, preach, exhort and comfort, because Jesus knew that man could not live by bread alone. Eventually

God's spirit within you will shrivel from lack of nourishment. And clawing their way through the space that once belonged to God are the villains that consumed your heart – unforgiveness and resentment.

Without consciously knowing it, I let these two vultures pick away at my insides for years. It wasn't until I was in my mid-thirties that I stopped running from my past, turned and looked back.

[1]Matthew 18:23-34, LB
[2]Jeremiah 31:34b, NAS
[3]Luke 6:37, author's paraphrase
[4]Luke 6:41, NAS
[5]Hebrews 10:25, author's paraphrase
[6]John 21:16c, KJ

# 9

# CONFESSIONS OF A FILE MANAGER

I began to see that throughout the trials of my life, I had never truly grieved. Early on, a pattern for survival was established; I created a filing cabinet in my mind. When I was hurt or angry, I shoved it in a drawer. When the drawer was full and would not hold anymore I locked it and opened a new one. My mother once said to me, "One thing about you is that you'll take more abuse than most, but when it's over, it's over. You never look back." But with my filing cabinet now full and bursting at the seams, I was forced to look back.

I opened each drawer, one at a time, and agonized over each painful experience. I was forced to face myself and the choices I had made in my life. For the first time in a very long time, I allowed myself to feel all the pain, all the fury and all the frustration. I did not allow myself the practiced luxury of blaming others. They were who they were and they had to deal with their own problems; I had to figure out why I had chosen such a self-destructive lifestyle.

I found I owed some people apologies. I wrote them letters, not asking them to return the favor, just owning up to sins against them. Other people I needed to forgive. Forgive, forget and go on. By God's grace I found myself able to do that, one person at a time. Eventually, all the drawers had been gone through. Some were empty but some were simply reorganized and in better order. I didn't realize it then, but so much of my identity was linked to those experiences that I simply refused to let them go. They were better organized now, and I was able to deal with them. But they were still there.

It took me three years to work through the pains of my life. During that time, I turned slowly back to God, one baby step at a time. I had found a church that did not threaten me. I even attended Sunday School class. For me, this was my first giant step. I was beginning to trust again. I enjoyed the class and was actually fond of the pastor of the church. But, after a couple of years, I felt a need to be in a single's program. My church hadn't yet started a singles' group, so I visited one that met in a local cafeteria on Sunday mornings. Wanting the group to be inter-denominational and attractive to those who might not enter a church building, the leaders had wisely chosen a non-threatening environment.

There were fifty-plus people on any given Sunday, and we were all in the same boat – single and needy. It was a wonderful time of sharing and growing, and for a season it was exactly what I needed to become whole again.

I had been so far away for so long, it was like starting over. But I was cautious. My new friends belonged to a charismatic Baptist church. Yeow!

"No thank you, I have my own church."

"No, really, I know you'd like me to visit, but I don't think so."

"Maybe next Sunday"

"Okay, okay, I'll go – just this once."

I was scared to death.

"Excuse me, but do y'all dance and stuff in the aisles?

No? Oh, good."

"Uh . . . what about that tongue thing? Never?" (Sigh of relief.)

When my questions were answered to my satisfaction, I went. But I discovered one question I forgot to ask. Hands . . . they raised their hands and swung them in the air! I felt *very* uneasy. But before long, I realized that I didn't have to raise *my* hands and I began to enjoy the celebration service replete with musical instruments and praise songs. This was a long way from solemn faces and silent services. I knew I could get into this!

But I remained extremely cautious. As I was trying out new friends in my new church, I stayed on the fringes. Not getting too involved, because I still didn't feel safe. My church wounds, raw through my twenties, were now only beginning to mend.

I also remained cautious of getting back into the Bible. Six years of don't, don't, don't at my former church was enough to convince me of that book's irrelevance to my life. An inspired book, full of wonderful parables and legends, written by men for the time in which they lived. That's what the Bible was. I did not believe it was to be taken literally. How could I? I had adjusted my personal doctrine a notch or two 'til I had a belief system that gave me room to move around. I still had not learned to give up control of my life. Jesus was my Savior, but I wasn't quite ready to give him control of my life.

I eventually met and married my wonderful husband Ronnie. This gentle, kind, loving man with two sons was just what I needed. Our new house became a home, exploding with all the energy and chaos four teenagers can generate.

Very early in my relationship with my incredibly perceptive husband, he learned something I didn't know. The largest drawer in the secret filing cabinet of my soul was hidden and locked up tight. The drawer I didn't know about was marked FATHER. I had only seen my father a half dozen times in my life. As a child, I dreaded his visits. Sitting on the front porch of my grandma's house, we didn't know what to say to each other.

"How's school?"

"Okay."

"What's your favorite subject?"

"English."

"Do you have any hobbies?"

"Reading, drawing," I would murmur without knowing how to expand any of my answers to take up more time. That finished, we would both stare down at our hands, embarrassed at the silence. I knew that he never sent child support, rarely sent Christmas or birthday presents and never acknowledged the school pictures mom sent year after year or the oil painting I was so proud of and had worked so hard on in my teens. After my first marriage, we stopped communicating altogether.

I had not seen nor heard from my father in nearly twenty years. "When we're in Albuquerque for the seminar, let's look up your dad," my husband Ronnie said casually.

"Oh sure. I can just see it. 'Dad, remember me? I'm your first born, Cheryl. Cheryl, that's C-H-E-R-Y-L, Cheryl. You don't? Well, that's okay, I know you've been busy.' I don't *think* so!"

Over the next several weeks, Ronnie brought it up again and again. "You could just call him while we're there. What could it hurt?"

"What could it hurt?" I shrieked, surprised at my depth of feeling.

"Look, I'm not calling that man, okay? He left my mom and me for another woman when I was six-months old. He didn't want me then and he doesn't want me now. Let's just drop it." But Ronnie didn't drop it, and the more he talked about it, the angrier I became.

He finally said, "We will never be able to have a really good relationship until you learn to forgive your father. You hate men because of what you think you know about him. It's time you found out what he's like for yourself." That stung. And hit a chord deep within me.

The next day I wrote and told my father we were coming to Albuquerque. If he wanted to see me, would he write me back? Weeks went by and I didn't receive an answer. *That figures.* Ronnie was more optimistic, "Maybe he moved. After all, it's been twenty years!" *If he doesn't live there, wouldn't the letter have been returned?*

The day we arrived in Albuquerque, Ronnie wanted me to call his home. "You want to meet him so badly, *you* call," I said.

"No, this is your dad, you call him."

My stomach was doing major flip-flops, and my

heart was bracing for rejection. Ring, ring, click. "Hello," my dad's voice sounding like it did when I was a kid.

"Dad, this is Cheryl, your daughter. My husband and I are in Albuquerque, we just arrived. Gee the weather's great," I rambled nervously.

"Hi! We were worried about you, glad you're here. How soon can we get together? Thought if you were free, we could go out for dinner tonight."

"Tonight?" I looked at Ronnie who was shaking his head yes. "Sure, sounds good," I lied.

That night was a splendid success. I've never loved my husband more. Generally quiet and shy around strangers, he took over the conversation providing an easing-in period for my father and me. We spent quite a bit of time with my dad and his wife over the next few days, and I was genuinely pleased to see the oil painting I had sent him so many years ago hanging in his living room. My stepmother, Paula, told me my dad was quite proud of it and had been showing it off to any new friends. We vowed upon leaving that we would call and see each other more often, which we did for the next several years, until I received a phone call from Paula saying my dad was ill.

I flew out that weekend. It was the first time since we had been reunited that I was going to see him without Ronnie. Nervous when I arrived at the airport, I debated about finding a hotel room before going to their house. They had not said anything about my staying there, so I hesitated to show up, bag in hand. But I decided to risk it and went straight to their house. "Of course we want you to stay here. We assumed you knew that! Don't be silly!" Paula said, as she guided me into the guest bedroom.

That weekend was the last time I saw my Dad. He

was very sick but strong enough to get around and enjoy company. We talked for hours, looking through family photo albums and getting to know each other. The day after he was buried I received the phone call. I didn't cry. Nor did I feel any real emotion other than a gentle sadness. I was thankful that Ronnie had insisted upon our reconciliation and will always be grateful for that encouragement.

In the three years my dad and I were reunited, I learned to forgive him. I realized that neither he nor Paula had intentionally ignored or slighted me. They lived in their own world, not answering letters, "assuming you would know." Not acknowledging love, but proudly hanging an oil painting done by a sixteen-year-old on the most prominent wall in their living room. They had filled a photo album with school pictures of a blonde, blue-eyed girl and displayed it on their entry table. My father, like many estranged dads, was filled with guilt. And all too often this guilt was assuaged with good intentions never fulfilled.

Through the healing process, I learned that over and over, from the time I was a little girl, I had searched for my dad. As I grew older, I found him in men who were domineering and abusive, men who drank too much, men who would reject me, men who would play out my expectations and validate my own low self-esteem. The self-destruction continued until well into my thirties I was able to look inward and by the grace of God find the hurting child who needed to experience unconditional love from a Father. My caring husband helped me find the courage to forgive and thereby find my life.

Finally, the filing cabinet was totally empty. Almost.

The remaining drawer, I discovered, was filled with

me. I had forgiven the church, and those in it who had filled my head and heart with nonsense. I had forgiven the men in my life who had abused me. I had forgiven friends along the way who had slighted or offended me. And finally I had forgiven my Dad. But I had not forgiven myself.

Many of us are harder on ourselves than we let on. On the surface we may appear to love our pothole as we wallow in the mire. But inside, we hate ourselves for being weak and out of control. And because we cannot forgive ourselves, we cannot imagine how God could. One thing that makes it so hard is that many of us, even though we hate our pit, cannot get out of it. And we are tired of asking for forgiveness when we know darn well that tomorrow or the next day we will be right back, doing the very thing we just asked to be forgiven for. So, we give up. And quit asking. But without forgiveness on the journey, we stumble and fall – again and again.

# 10

# MORE, BIGGER, WIDER, LONGER, HIGHER

**Idolatry**
Worship of idols, excessive devotion to or reverence for some person or thing.

Idolatry is a word seldom used in modern times. However, by definition it's as fashionable as a new Mercedes. And it is this pink and green plaid-lined ditch that has became the home of many twentieth-century Christians who stumbled over greed and envy.

In the Old Testament, God warned the Israelites about the dangers of idol worship. You probably remember the story that showed how well they listened. The Israelites were led out of Egyptian slavery and away from the tyranny of Pharaoh by Moses (Charlton Heston). God opened the Red Sea so his children could walk safely to their promised land. He was a visible presence on their journey – a cloud by day, a pillar of fire by night. And after seeing all these miraculous wonders performed by God, the Israelites had memory failure. As soon as Moses' back was turned, they built a golden calf. When Moses came down the mountain with the Ten Commandments, he saw the people worshipping their idol.

Back then, idols were really crazy things like animals, weird looking statues of women with their parts in the wrong places, insects . . . you name it. These idols represented transferred devotion – from the God of heaven and earth – to a graven image. And the image was always molded by the hands of humans.

Today idols nestle somewhat closer to our hearts and become the object of our devotion. Few of us go to the trouble of melting down our fine jewels to craft an idol. We simply pull out a credit card or go to a bank. Then we wax, gas-up, tinker, count, dust and do our worship thing. Of course, idols are not always inanimate objects. Sometimes they breathe and suck the life from us. Whatever they are, our idols of choice become our identity and take on the shape of our heart.

Idolatry sneaks up so quietly that most Christians don't see it coming. After all, our possessions are not bad, in and of themselves. The danger lies in how we respond to them and how we allow them to affect us. I have a friend who showed me how *not* to respond. Michelle is now a woman in her early forties, with two beautiful children, a storybook home and a broken heart.

Michelle met David when they were in college. They dated off and on through her junior year, fell in love in her senior year and married after her graduation. Michelle adored David, even though her parents had never approved of him. They liked David well enough but recognized some potential problems in the relationship that love

110

might not overcome. While Michelle was a born-again believer, David was not. But Michelle was convinced this was her man and that he would become a Christian soon.

For the first few months, David kept his promise and went to church with Michelle, but as time went on his attendance became erratic. Tired of going alone, Michelle gave in and soon began staying home on Sunday morning with her handsome husband to enjoy eggs over easy and the Sunday paper. Gradually Michelle lost touch with her Christian friends. Then she stopped reading her Bible. Soon David's friends and priorities became hers. His time became consumed with making money. Her time was spent climbing the social ladder, doing volunteer work.

I occasionally ran into Michelle at a community event and heard about her shopping trips to Europe, her redecorating projects, her new Mercedes and her condo on the coast. The last time I saw her I knew immediately that something was very wrong. She looked as though her world had disintegrated before her very eyes, and in truth it had. Feeling bitter and betrayed, she confessed that she and David were separated and involved in a nasty divorce settlement. The life she had chosen had turned against her. The husband she had given up everything for had abandoned her for a younger bride. And as she looked back over her life, she wondered what had gone wrong.

I believe that in her heart, Michelle knows that she has *chosen* a life without God. But Michelle is a prideful person. She is someone who would rather place blame than search out and confront the inner issues. Admitting to herself that her problems stem from the choices *she* made would be the first step in Michelle's recovery. She would see that she allowed her husband to be the center of her universe and the objects she coveted her graven images. But she is not ready to take responsibility. Michelle now blames God for letting her world fall apart. Isn't that just like a human?

The Bible is clear. God wants our devotion, our love and our obedience – anything less is not worthy of the death of his only Son. But the really amazing thing about God is that he never gives up on us. Even when we waste years scurrying around collecting and loving our stuff, he waits. Even though he knows that the life he planned for us is far superior to the life we're choosing, he waits. And when we come to our senses and realize that nothing in this world comes close to filling the yearning of our soul, he is there.

One of the most beautiful word pictures in the Bible is found in the Gospel of Matthew, where through the voice of the Son, we hear how the heart of the Father longed for the return of His chosen people. (Remember, these were the Israelites who time and time again disappointed him. No matter what God did for them, it was never enough.)

"Oh Jerusalem, Jerusalem . . .
How often I wanted to gather your children together,
the way a hen gathers her chicks under her wings,
and you were unwilling."[1]

Anyone who has longed for a wayward child or an estranged spouse to return home, understands the grief this verse conveys. Here is the God of heaven and earth, the creator of the universe, the giver and taker of all life, comparing his feelings to those of a loving hen wanting to protect her chicks. What kind of a God is this? What kind of love is this? He is a God whose love is completely beyond our comprehension.

When Michelle is able to stare into the mirror and lock eyes with her own reflection, she will begin to see what she has done. She will see the things she has collected for what they are – only things. She will understand that a husband cannot take the place of God. Then, and only then, will Michelle be broken. And God will be there, ready to wrap his wings of love and protection around his little girl.

God does not expect us to live in self-styled poverty, nor do I think he wants us to live in opulence while others are in need. He has placed us where he wants us to be – to be used by him in our family, our neighborhood, our city and our country. He expects us to be content in whatever situation he has chosen to place us. If he has given you wealth, you need not feel guilty. The problem is not the things we have but the value we place on our things. And whether we place our trust in our things, our money, our relationships or our God. It all goes back to the Boulevard of Control. Idolatry is one of the potholes along the way. When a Christian yanks authority away from God and follows after the things of his own heart, he finds himself serving a ruthless master. He will never have enough things, nor feel enough love. This is when envy rears its ugly head – the keeping-up-with-the-Joneses syndrome. And when he catches up with the Joneses will he be content to stay equal? Unfortunately for him there will always be the Smiths and the Kendricks with more. And one more hill to climb.

I was listening to a Christian radio show recently and heard the commentator tell of a young woman who had come to him for advice. She was upset that her husband insisted she go back to work after the birth of their second child. She was so distraught about leaving her children in day care that she broke down while talking to this sympathetic counselor. A week later, on a whim, the counselor drove by this woman's house. He told the radio audience how shocked he was to see a 4,000 square foot home in an upscale neighborhood. In front of the house were two expensive, new vehicles.

No wonder the woman had to work. And you can bet she had something to do with the size of the home and the expense of the cars. Too bad she hadn't prioritized the desires of her heart sooner.

Here's the bottom line: Christians choose slavery when they allow the things they buy to determine their priorities. Carefully define your priorities and you will have no problem determining which purchases should be made. Until you do that your life will not be your own.

We all have decisions to make each day. Do we buy? Do we save? Do we watch TV? Do we play with our kids? We only have so much money in the bank and so many hours in a day. Each dollar comes with responsibility. Each hour begins with a question mark.

¹Matthew 23:37, NAS

# 11

# WHO ME? NO WAY!

**Fear**
A feeling of anxiety and agitation caused by the presence or nearness of danger, evil, pain, etc.; timidity; dread; terror; fright; apprehension.

You will probably remember our next prodigal, because he was a disciple. This robust fisherman was chosen by Jesus as one of the twelve men who would follow him throughout his three years of ministry. Peter was quite a character. One evening while the disciples were in a fishing boat on the Sea of Galilee they saw Jesus walking across the water toward them. They thought he was a ghost, but Jesus reassured them and told them not to be afraid. Before the other disciples could react, Peter, full of vim and vigor and lots of faith, had climbed out of the boat and started walking *on the water* toward Jesus! When Peter realized what he was doing, he looked down and started to sink. That was Peter.

Peter pulled quite a stunt in the Garden of Gethsemane. For three years Peter had heard Jesus preach peace and prophesy about his arrest and death. But when the guards came to arrest Jesus, Peter forgot. He drew his sword and cut off a guard's ear. He might have been killed if Jesus hadn't immediately healed the injured man.

In the Upper Room, Peter swore to Jesus his undying love, but Jesus knew Peter's weakness. He told Peter that before the cock crowed, he would deny ever having known him. And that is just what happened.

After Jesus was arrested, Peter went into the city to see what would happen to his friend. He was hanging around outside warming his hands by a fire, when someone said, "Aren't you a friend of the guy they just arrested?"

"Who me? No way!"

Two more times someone asked him, and two more times he denied knowing Jesus. And as Jesus was being led away, he turned to look at Peter and together they heard the cock crow. Can you imagine how Peter felt? The Bible says, "he went out and wept bitterly."[1] Fear had caused him to deny the one to whom he had declared undying love only hours before.

Fear has caused many Christians to deny Christ. In America, we don't fear martyrdom; we fear ridicule. Today Christians who stand firm in Christ's teachings are not popular. We are called right-wing, anti-choice and intolerant. While liberal, humanistic views have free reign in our society, Christian views are being censored. We hand our children money with "In God We Trust" printed in bold letters, recite "One nation, under God" in saying the Pledge of Allegiance and then remind them not to pray at school. It's illegal, you know.

And what about our businesses and corporations? How popular is it to announce to your fellow workers that you are a born-again Christian?

Some months ago, I was having lunch with a business associate from Dallas. In the course of our conversation, she asked me if it was hard to live my faith in the business environment. Without hesitation, I said to her, "Once I determined to learn what God expects from me in his Word, living my faith in any environment came as naturally as life itself." But, I own my own business, so I set the standards. I asked her the same question. She confided that her career situation made it almost impossible for her to keep her job and maintain her principles. She didn't know what to do because the management of her company expected her to lie to customers. While she liked her job, she might be forced to leave it. And she was afraid the next company might be worse than the first. And she is right . . . it might be. But my advice to her that day came from lessons I had learned as a Christian businesswoman: "Standing firm for what you believe takes courage. But it is never the wrong decision if you are on the side of God."

Another form of fear comes from our need for acceptance. We want others to like us. So, sometimes it feels easier to pretend that our Christianity is a private matter. I have a friend whose big, macho son, Craig was saved awhile back. He works in the construction field with some tough men who swear a lot and tell off-color jokes. Craig was too afraid to tell anyone that his life had changed. He kept his salvation a secret, for fear of being laughed at. Consequently, not much changed for Craig. He goes along with his pack of buds, laughs at their jokes and keeps the fact that he is a child of the King a secret.

What do we fear? Peter feared being identified with

a man who had just been arrested. Possibly he feared for his own life. Or maybe, just for a short time, Peter began having doubts and did not want to be known as a man who followed an impostor. If Jesus was who he said he was, why didn't he do something? Peter had been an eye-witness to hundreds of miracles performed by Jesus . . . were they tricks? How could Roman guards have the power of life and death over the Son of God? Peter's doubts and fears would have been put to rest if he knew then what we know now. Just a few days later, Jesus rose from the grave and showed the world that his Father's power was stronger than man's greatest fear, death.

Two-thousand years later, we have all the facts. We know the resurrection story and yet many are still afraid. Many deny Christ every day in words and by their actions.

Are we afraid because we are ashamed of our faith, or because of what it has been reduced to in our lives, and in the world? If every Christian followed the teachings of Jesus, we would have a faith to be proud of. We could never build enough church buildings for all the people clamoring to get into them. Obviously, that is not happening. Every time a televangelist takes a nose dive, the rest of us suffer for it. We have all heard comments like, "It didn't surprise me. Those guys are all in it for the money . . . that's why they're preachers. You Christians are all a bunch of hypocrites." And so we hide our faith . . . in fear.

There is good news for all the scaredy-cats out there. *It's never too late to find courage.* If you have denied Christ, in word or action, you are no different from Peter. And guess what? Jesus lovingly forgave Peter. The first sign we see of this forgiveness is a treasure tucked away in Mark's account of the empty tomb. Remember, this takes place *after* Peter denied Christ. Mary Magdalene (the former hooker) went with a couple of friends to Jesus' tomb to anoint his body. It was gone! An angel appeared to the women and said, "Go, tell his disciples **and Peter**, he is going before you into Galilee; there you will see him, just as he said to you." [2] Isn't that something Jesus would do? Can you see him now – "Listen, angel, I want you to deliver a message for me. Go to my tomb and let the disciples know where I'll be. Oh, and by the way, I know Peter is feeling down on himself, so make sure he knows that he should come too." Do you think Jesus was angry with Peter? Sure doesn't sound like it to me.

Peter went on to be a dynamic, courageous leader in the early church. In the midst of Roman and Jewish persecution, under the threat of death, Peter went from house to house giving his eye-witness account of the life, death and resurrection of Jesus. He went from village to village performing miracles and healing the sick. And finally, inspired by the Holy Spirit, he wrote two books of God's holy Word, the Bible.

Courage comes from the Holy Spirit who indwells each believer's life. Without the Holy Spirit, Peter was a wuss. He denied Christ then cried like a baby. The Holy Spirit was not scheduled to make his appearance until after Christ died. Prior to the crucifixion, Jesus told his disciples, "But I tell you the truth, it is to your advantage that I go away; for if I do not go away, the Helper shall not come to you; but if I go, I will send him to you. . . . But when he, the Spirit of truth, comes, he will guide you into all the truth."[3] The book of Acts describes how after Jesus' resurrection, his believers were all filled with the

Holy Spirit. Then and only then, Peter became a man of courage.

God does not expect any of us to be courageous without his help. And the secret to gaining his help is to admit you can't be brave by yourself. "In your weakness, I am made strong,"[4] he tells us in the Bible. It is not surprising to God that you are afraid, nor that you do not want to be embarrassed. He knows our weaknesses . . . much better than we do. All he asks of us is an obedient, yielded heart, and he will do the rest. The more of yourself you yield to him, the more courage you will have to stand. But yielding and admitting you are weak are problems for many. It is a little matter called pride.

[1]Matthew 26:75b, KJ
[2]Mark 16:7, NAS
[3]John 16:7,13a, NAS
[4]II Corinthians 12:9, author's paraphrase

# 12

# KUDOS TO JIM BAKKER AND KING NEB!

**Pride**
An over-high opinion of oneself; exaggerated self-esteem; conceit.

The younger brother in the prodigal story started out with pride, but the older brother never got rid of it. Both were led into deception because of it.

I was raised in a Christian home, but for some reason pride was taught as a virtue instead of as a sin. I remember hearing, "Where's your pride, young lady? Don't let them see you cry. Hold your head up." It has taken years for me to understand that pride puts a barrier between me and others. It provides the mortar for the bricks that become my wall of defense. Pride is the source of many of our problems with God and most of our problems with each other. We are too proud to admit we are wrong, too proud to say we are sorry, too proud to ask for forgiveness, too proud to tell our kids we made a mistake, too proud to admit we are less than perfect in our Christian walk and too proud to ask for help. God hates pride. The Bible tells us that "Pride goes before destruction, and a haughty spirit before stumbling."[1] Life experience proves this true. Just look at the number of prideful people who are on top of the world one minute and on scandal sheets the next.

In the Bible, God tells us that "the craze for sex, the ambition to buy everything that appeals to you, and the pride that comes from wealth and importance – these are not from God. They are from this evil world itself."[2] Interesting that these are the major problems in marriages today, destroying families and ruining relationships. Satan must love it when we buy into his standards instead of God's. Why do we do this?

Have you ever known you were wrong, but could not for the life of you blurt out those three little words that someone desperately needed to hear . . . *I am sorry?* Somehow many of us have mistaken these words as a sign of weakness instead of strength. Our politicians seem to think it is much better to deny the truth than to break down and admit they were wrong. Many times I have thought how nice it would be if a president, or senator, or anyone in an exalted position were to face up to the American people and admit he had made a mistake. Instead, our exalted ones give us gobbledygook. And what is worse, they insult our intelligence by operating under the assumption that we're buying into their lies and half-truths. Of course, by now we are so disillusioned we might not believe the truth if and when we hear it. We might even be too cynical to appreciate a truthful confession. But I, for one, wanted the opportunity to hear at least one brave soul admit guilt before I die.

Jim Bakker has given me that opportunity. Though not a politician, Jim Bakker was a popular televanglist and head of a multi-million dollar ministry. Through the media, the world learned of his demise. I have to admit I was never a fan of his and was not all that surprised when his ministry came toppling down on top of him and Tammy Faye. When he received a forty-five year prison sentence, I thought it was overkill, but did not understand all the charges against him, so I assumed it was justified. After that, I thought little about him.

While in a bookstore, I saw his book, *I Was Wrong*. Intrigued by the title, I picked it up, saw how thick it was and put it down. I walked to the front of the store intending to leave but something pulled me back. I bought the book, took it home and read into the night. Each evening for the next few days, I read nonstop. At times I was crying so hard I had to put it down. Other times I paused to contemplate the intensity of the pain captured in the words. When I finished reading the account of Jim Bakker's life, I felt I knew the man. And there was no doubt in my mind that he was sincere. Yes, he was wrong in many, many ways. And he was too prideful to see it for too many years. But when God locked the door to his cell and finally got his attention, Jim Bakker broke. Humbled in every way that is humanly possible, he came out of prison a repentant and forgiven man.

In his book, he did not try to justify his actions. He revealed his sins and to the world said, "I was wrong." That took courage, humility and character. And for that, he is a man I will forever admire and respect.

Too many Christians have robed themselves in the world's prideful values. We have forgotten that when we are weak, God is strong. Too often in times of desperate need when we should be depending totally on God, we draw our strength from sheer will, determined to show no vulnerability. It is extremely difficult for many of us to appear weak. We believe that someone will take advantage of us and we'll lose control of the situation. Instead of drawing strength from God, we pat ourselves on the back for being self-sufficient. Totally in control. Arrogant, haughty and completely conformed to the world. We strut our stuff and call the shots.

There is a terrific story in the Bible about a king who found out how much God hates pride. His name was Nebuchadnezzar and he was the mighty king of Babylon (present-day Iraq).

To give you some background, God had warned the Israelites for centuries that unless they shaped up he would send a foreign king after them. Then came King Neb. Not only did he capture the sacred city of Jerusalem, but he took from it everything of value, including the young men. (Enter Daniel, Shadrach, Meshach and Abed-nego.) These kids, especially Daniel, became great friends of the king.

When King Neb had strange dreams, which he seemed to have often, God gave Daniel a supernatural ability to interpret them. One such dream foretold history from 605 B.C. till the end of time. In this dream, King Neb saw a huge statue of a man made out of gold, silver, bronze, iron and clay. When asked what this meant, Daniel told the king that the gold head was the Babylonian empire and then went on to tell about future empires represented by the other metals and materials. The dream showed that God was in control and had a plan mapped out for the nations. Daniel told the king who would rule, when and how, until the Messiah's second coming – at which time all the nations would be destroyed.

So what would any self-respecting king do? King Neb had a ninety-foot tall by nine-foot wide gold statue made of himself. And then commanded everyone to bow down and worship it. When Daniel's friends would not, he threw them into a fiery furnace. You probably remember that they came out of it just fine. Much better than King Neb did, in fact.

I titled the next chapter of Daniel, "God severely pruned Neb." After countless warnings from God and pleas to repent from Daniel, King Nebuchadnezzar "was driven away from mankind and began eating grass like cattle, and his body was drenched with the dew of heaven, until his hair had grown like eagles' feathers and his nails like birds' claws." And he stayed like that for seven years.

Afterward, in the king's own hand he wrote:
"But at the end of that period, I Nebuchadnezzar, raised my eyes toward heaven and my reason returned to me, and I blessed the Most High and praised and honored Him who lives forever . . . . At that time my reason returned to me. And my majesty and splendor were restored to me . . . *and surpassing greatness was added to me.* Now I, Nebuchadnezzar praise, exalt, and honor the King of heaven, for all His works are true and His ways just, and **He is able to humble those who walk in pride.**"[3]

This a wonderful story of the faithfulness of God in the face of human arrogance. Yes, King Neb suffered for his boastful pride, but God allowed the suffering for one reason

– to bring him back to himself. When that was accomplished, God not only restored all that the king had, he added surpassing greatness. God does not delight in punishing his children. He does it because he loves us and wants us to return to him. And while discipline is not what we would choose for ourselves, "whom the Lord loves he disciplines."[4]

[1]Proverbs 16:18, NAS
[2]I John 2:16, LB
[3]Daniel 4:33-34, 36-37, NAS (emphasis added)
[4]Hebrews 12:6a, NAS

# 13

# THE BRIAR PATCH

**Worldliness**
The condition or quality of being worldly (devoted to or concerned with the affairs and pleasures of the world).

Here is a biggie. Many prodigals can claim this one, including yours truly. As I strutted down the Boulevard of Control I stumbled on pleasures and tripped over my own understanding. Before I knew it, I belly flopped into one of the deepest canyons of all.

There is no doubt that the world itself is a beautiful place; God has given us much to enjoy. It's not the place that's the problem, nor the stuff in the place. It's what we do with the stuff that creates a problem for us!

When I was young, I wondered why God had so many don'ts. It seemed sadistic that he would give us all the pleasures in the world and then tell us, "Don't touch!" As I matured, I realized the things God did not want us to do in the world were not good for us. But it is hard convincing young people in the party-prime of their life.

I wrote the following some time back when I was

trying to express my fascination with the seedy side of life.

*The world holds a glorious allure for a season, just as the bright lights of Las Vegas beckon from miles away on the highway or in the sky. But as you draw closer to those lights that seem so fascinating from a distance, they become blinders to reality. With no depth of conscience, the surface becomes its own importance. And as you glide on its glassy facade, overwhelmed with pleasure, you forget that beneath the filmy surface lie the pitfalls to hell.*

In this generation we should know that. We have seen the destructiveness of greed. We've seen the result of promiscuous sex. The near extinction of the family brought on by lust, selfishness and anger. The chaos wrought by lawlessness. We see all the signs and yet we continue to glide along carelessly, hoping against hope that things will get better. But things won't get better until we learn to take God seriously.

God created the world as sort of a testing ground. After Adam and Eve blew it, they were kicked out of the garden. Sin entered the picture and God's most beautiful angel Lucifer – turned devil – was given free reign over the world. That is why the Bible tells us not to be conformed to this world but to separate ourselves from it. If you give Satan an inch, I can assure you he will take as many miles as he can. It is not a pretty picture.

But many of God's children are so tangled up in the world, we are no longer willing to turn away from it. After tasting earthly pleasures, we discover that our appetite is insatiable. Soon these immoral and unhealthy morsels have become a way of life. We have embraced a lifestyle that has taken hold and nudged its way into our hearts.

I for one liked being out in the world. I was foot-loose in the 70s — when free love and drugs went main-stream. I went along with my friends — living it up and liv-ing for self. At the time, I could justify everything I did. I was not a horrible person, I was just your average twenty-something doing what came naturally.

I didn't know it then, but God was always there. Not just on those rare days when I felt his presence, but always. Some days I took God to bars and got drunk. Some nights I laid him next to someone I barely knew. He was taken to places where people damned his name and swore by his Son. He was there. His grieving Spirit was there all along. And I did not know.

Because we prodigals are wise in our own eyes, we begin formulating a belief system that fits our lifestyle and conforms to our submerged conscience. Pretty soon we are convinced that intelligent people do not really believe the Bible — it is for the weak, those who need a crutch.

We are okay when we are busy, so we become workaholics or we join more committees. We buy lots of stuff. Quiet isn't good, because we have to think, so we play music or leave the TV on even when we are not watching it. Noise, that's what we need. Noise and lots of people. So we go to bars and parties — anywhere, anything to drown out the guilt and the self-accusations. Sure, we find lots of people who agree with us. "Life is for living — go for the gusto." "You only go around once."

They feast in our failings . . . misery loves company.

We read in the Bible a principle that lives itself out in human experience, you cannot serve two masters. There's no middle ground, no fence to sit on. It's either one way or the other. You either love this world and all that is in it, or you love God. You either live for making a name for yourself on earth, or you live for the jewels in your crown in heaven. You either serve Satan, or you serve God. By not choosing, you serve Satan by default.

God has warned us that Satan has dominion over the earth. After that little incident in the garden, God took dominion from man and turned it over to Satan. We are told that God's children are aliens in this world, strangers in a strange land. Our citizenship is in heaven, our lives a vapor of steam. Our journey through Satan's domain is thankfully short and many times acutely painful. While unbelievers trivialize Satan, and the-devil-made-me-do-it jokes poke fun at the concept of an evil one with powers of infinite destruction, Christians who are living for God quake at the havoc this fallen angel has wrought. Peter sent out a warning when he said, "Be on the alert! Your adversary, the devil, prowls about like a roaring lion, seeking someone to devour."[1] And let me tell you, we prodigals stuck in our potholes are an easy target.

God wants to protect his children and keep us from the hurts of the world. But when we choose to live without God, we put ourselves in a position of weakness, playing into Satan's crafty plans. Our struggles on earth are never as they appear to be on the surface. The Bible tells us that "For our struggle is not against flesh and blood, but against the rulers, against the powers, against the world forces of this darkness, against the spiritual forces of wickedness in the heavenly places."[2] There is a war raging all around us, the war of good against evil. I know that if God opened our eyes to the battles being fought for our souls, every man, woman and child would run for cover. But we can't see.

God doesn't work like that. He doesn't scare us into submission, instead in his divine love and wisdom he gave us the gift of free will. We have been given the right to choose based on faith – "the certainty that what we hope for is waiting for us, even though we cannot see it up ahead."[3] God desires that all his creations flee from Satan and run to him. He desires that "whoever believes in (Jesus) should not perish but have eternal life."[4]

But he isn't a God who interferes.

He lets us choose the path

for our life's journey . . .

and for all eternity.

[1]I Peter 5:8b, NAS
[2]Ephesians 6:12, NAS
[3]Hebrews 11:1b, LB
[4]John 3:16b, NAS

# 14

# GOD LOVES YOU, FAULTS & ALL!

**Guilt**
Synonyms: remorse, repentance, self-condemnation, self-accusation.

While the Bible doesn't explore the subject of guilt in either the story of the younger brother, or the story of David, you can be sure guilt played havoc on both men.

A sensitive conscience is a God-given gift. In the book of Jeremiah, God said, "I will put my law within them and on their heart I will write it; and I will be their God, and they shall be my people."[1] Not only can we know right from wrong, God has given us a way to *feel* the difference. When we cannot trust our natural urges, our conscience becomes our guide. That is the theory, anyway. Unfortunately not all of us are good followers. Some of us prefer to lead. And that is when we get into trouble. Ignoring our conscience guide, we blaze through new territory and do something we know we should not do.

Although God is not pleased, He is not surprised. God knows us and he is well acquainted with our faults – not only the ones we had yesterday, but the ones we will develop ten years from now. As a human, I cannot fathom how that is possible, but it is a fact. Time is of earth, not of eternity. So way back then when God looked into the future, he knew King David was going to fall – big time! Did he then decide to chose another king for his people, one who would not disappoint and embarrass him? No, he stuck with David, faults and all.

Knowing that we humans cannot possibly be perfect, God sent his Son to die for our sins. At *that* moment our sins were forgiven and will be remembered no more. When I became a believer, God sent his Holy Spirit to inhabit my life. I then had new power to overcome sin. By yielding my own desires to God's desires, I would sin less and less. When I did sin, his plan remained perfect. I felt so bad about sinning against God that I immediately repented and the weight of my guilt was lifted. The closer I stayed to him, the fewer temptations came my way and when they did come, I had power to say no. It is a perfect plan of salvation and sanctification.

But when I started moving away from God and took back control of my life, I created my own plan. I did what I wanted, with little or no thought of the consequences. There were times when my conscience got the best of me and I sincerely wanted to change and return to the peace I had found in my early years as a Christian. But each time I tried, the shame of guilt got in the way. I no longer felt forgiven. Because of my unbelief, the stakes of sin disappeared, but the canvas of guilt remained. It shielded my eyes from God and prevented my fellowship with him.

Satan loves when we allow this to happen. And I allowed him to deceive me by painting my past mistakes onto my canvas of guilt so that any time I tried to talk to God all I saw was how unworthy I was. I began thinking my sins were so huge that God couldn't possibly have really forgiven me. Beaten down, I lived a life of defeat until I chose to break free.

Choosing to break free is a conscious decision. It doesn't just happen. It took me years to figure that out. I tried and failed so many times in my life, I doubted if I could ever live free of shame and guilt. It was not until I took the time and effort to learn what grace actually meant, that I understood. Seeing sin and forgiveness from God's perspective was one of the most freeing experiences of my life.

When Jesus came to earth he brought with him a whole new way of looking at and understanding sin. Being the radical of his day, he alienated the Jewish leaders by first ignoring, then challenging, the traditional laws they held sacred. Those who thought themselves righteous because they had kept the religious law were called hypocrites by the Son of God. He had no use for their self-congratulatory piety. Yet the adulterous woman who would have been stoned to death was spared as her remorse touched the compassionate heart of Jesus.

His revolutionary teachings of sin and forgiveness wiped out any shred or hope of man's self-righteousness and made Jesus a hated adversary of the religious leaders of the day. Jesus saw through their rhetoric and spoke words that drove deep into the heart of the listener. He knew that the religious leaders put more credence in following petty laws than in loving God or their fellow man. They made a big to-do about eating only kosher food, but ignored the fact that many around them had no food. When Jesus told them they had missed the point, his disciples were all in a stew because Jesus had offended these religious leaders. Jesus didn't much care. He said, "Don't you understand? Don't you see that anything you eat passes through the digestive tract and out again? But evil words come from an evil heart, and defile the man who says them. For from the heart come evil thoughts, murder, adultery, fornication, theft, lying and slander. These are what defile. . . "[2]

It is interesting that these sins were grouped together. We have already discovered that Jesus considered a man who was angry without cause as guilty before the courts as the man who commits murder. Now we see that lying is as bad as stealing. But are these sins of the mind really as terrible as adultery and fornication? Jesus made no distinction. To God, sin is sin and all sin is evil in his sight. Jesus taught that anything a person thought or did that was not done in love and did not bring glory and honor to the Father was sin.

Many think as long as they only do the small sins like gossiping and telling "little white lies" they are okay. They go on their merry way thinking they have lived a righteous life. Those who have succumbed to the "really bad" sins think they are less loved by God and use as a standard of measure those they see as more spiritual. God alone is the judge and he weighs the heart. He is as ready to forgive the murderer, the adulterer and the thief as he is the church deacon who passes along gossip in the form of a prayer request.

The bottom line is that God wants to commune

with his children. Sin of any kind keeps us from being in total communication with our Father until we come to him broken and humble . . . seeking his will.

In a small church group recently, the question was posed "What is your struggle with sin and how do you deal with it?" An insightful friend, who I knew had spent many years living a life similar to the younger brother in the prodigal son story, answered, "My struggle has mainly been in moving from believing that the Christian life is about overcoming sin, to a belief that it's about a relationship with Jesus, and that sin is just a distraction." That statement was so profound, I spent the next week pondering it. Of all the struggles she could have shared, she chose the one closest to God's heart. We are to stop focusing on past mistakes and focus on the heart of Christianity – a relationship with Jesus. God wants us to move on. But many of us become so bogged down in guilt, we are immobilized.

To the believer, all sin is a heavy weight that can be used by the demon king. He deceives us into believing that we're not good enough, that we'll never measure up to what God expects, so why bother? He uses our guilt and shame to build a wall separating us from God. The higher the wall, the harder it is to tear it down and feel God's mercy. We hide away in our self-made prisons somehow thinking that God doesn't see us anymore – or hear us. As Satan feeds us his lies, we begin doubting the blacks and whites of our spiritual existence. Manipulating truth to suit our own purposes, we become wise in our own eyes.

I know because I've been there. The longer I lived in a world I created through sin, the harder it was for me to hear the truth or to understand that God still loved me and would welcome me back into His arms.

As a warning to those who might see this as a loophole for committing sin, let me tell you, my journey back was not an easy one. It took me almost twenty years of heartbreak and suffering. It is not easy to break through the chains of bondage. I had given Satan such a stronghold in my life, I felt powerless to overcome the waves of temptation that came to me daily.

I know that during this time of my life God was no less powerful than he is today, but I had the responsibility of crawling my way back to him. He didn't supernaturally make everything right. The choices I had made in my disobedience cost me dearly. Looking back, I know he was there all along and I know he shielded me from many things that could have happened to me. But he let me crawl on my baby legs, gradually finding the strength to stand . . . then walk, in his full presence and infinite mercy.

Is all guilt bad? Not by a long shot. If you feel guilt, it shows that your conscience is still sensitive to God. You are one of the more fortunate prodigals. Many have passed by this pothole without so much as a stumble. Their conscience is long gone, or so it would appear. The Bible says it a lot more eloquently: "But the Holy Spirit tells us clearly that in the last times some in the church will turn away from Christ and become eager followers of teachers with devil-inspired ideas. These teachers will tell lies with straight faces and do it so often that their consciences won't even bother them."[3] We are being warned – if you play with fire, you are going to get burned. The lies that you buy into will sear your conscience. And that is what has happened to those who feel no guilt and shame.

What makes guilt a pothole is you, and how you choose to deal with it. If you allow it to keep you from returning to God, then yes . . . it is bad. If you allow it to convict your heart and effect change, guilt is good.

My daughter, Jayne, worked for Life Outreach International, a ministry that produces the Christian talk show, "Life Today with James Robison." Many of the programs deal with Christian restoration – they called these segments "Set Free." Last year, they did a piece on sexual addiction. Part of Jayne's job as an associate producer was to find people willing to go on national television and tell their stories. She approached this show with apprehension – afraid she would be unable to find Christians willing to admit that they were addicted to sex. By the time the showed aired, Jayne was amazed how many came forward. For weeks thereafter, letters from people crying out for help, poured into the ministry. Of course, I am not privy to these confidential appeals, but my daughter told me that they were from people from all walks of life . . . people riddled by guilt and shame. They expressed surprise that others were being held hostage by sexual addiction. They drew courage from knowing that they were not alone. This courage provided the power to reach out of their pothole of guilt . . . and seek help and forgiveness.

It is human to hide when we are guilty. You don't want your darkness exposed to the light. You don't want others to see who you really are. But with all prodigals hiding away, you begin to think you must be the only one doing the things you do. There were times in my life, when I walked into a church and thought everyone there was a spiritual giant, except me. I walked out of church feeling only condemnation. Not because of anything anyone said, only because of my guilty conscience. I would never have dreamed of sharing the shames of my life with a spiritual giant. Since then, I have become friends with some of those I considered more spiritual than me. As we began to trust each other and share experiences, I found more than one friend with a past she's not proud of. Many have weaknesses that haunt them today. I no longer look at them and see spiritual giants. I see men and women honestly seeking after God. And I see them growing as he shows them areas in their lives that need to change.

On my journey, I came slowly to understand that while we won't talk about it, most of us have things we would like to hide. And so many think others are better than they.

This idea of the "super Christian" came home to me one Sunday morning while attending the singles' group I mentioned earlier. By this time, the group had been meeting for over a year. We had been on retreats together and had truly bonded. There were not many secrets between us. While a few romances bloomed, on the whole, we hung out as a group learning to trust again.

One lady who was new to the city and had never heard our stories held up her hand during a discussion time and said, "I have a horrible sin in my life. I'm too ashamed to even tell you what it is. I'm afraid you won't accept me." Thinking she must be a mass murderer or a porno star, we held our breath, almost afraid to hear her confession. Someone finally said, "It's okay, this is a group that is open and honest and loving. We won't hold anything against you. We too, are finding our way and when we slip and fall, we're here to support each other."

With that the lady slowly reached into her purse and silently held up a pack of cigarettes. "That's it? You smoke?"

I asked in my best Barbra Streisand voice. I then reached into my purse and held up my cigarettes as did several others. (Of course, that was before smoking was worse than starring in porno flicks in many people's minds; before I, as well as most of the others, have since quit.)

Here was a lady who almost did not come to our singles meeting because she was convinced her sin was too great and she would be shunned by other, "more spiritual" Christians.

Unfortunately, I understood too well what this woman was going through. There was a time in my life that I believed that no one could possibly be as bad as I was. I had just joined the singles' group and signed up to go on a retreat. The first night, the very wise leader asked us to write down our five worst sins, put the list in a sealed envelope and hand them in. Even though we were not to sign our names, I feared he would be able to recognize my handwriting so I purposely wrote with a backhand slope to my letters.

The next day in a large conference room overlooking Lake Livingston, I held my breath. What if he recognized that list as mine? Did I notice him looking at me in a strange way? (Am I paranoid or what?) When it came time to discuss our lists, I was amazed when he said that all of us had listed essentially the same sins or variations on the same themes. None of the sins were much different than the others. I began to look around the room at the faces of people who I imagined to be better Christians than I. If we all struggled with essentially the same problems, why didn't we talk about them? Others must have felt the same way I did, because that retreat brought us close together and forged open and honest friendships that are precious to me to this day.

Being able to tell you the truth about myself shows me how much I have grown. I no longer care if you judge me – that is your pothole, not mine. While I am certainly not proud of my past, I see it as that . . . my past. I no longer feel guilty, because I know that I have been forgiven. I repented and in repenting I changed directions. I am no longer on the detour road, and the potholes are far behind. I have been set free. "You shall know the truth, and the truth shall make you free."[4]

When I was deep into my potholes, I did not care that I could no longer see the light that once had illuminated my journey map. I made up my own truth. I did not need a map. There were plenty of other people to show me the way. But after awhile I grew weary. I discovered that potholes and ditches do not have roads, they have ruts. And all of us who fooled ourselves into thinking we were going somewhere were actually stuck in ruts, traveling in circles. The longer and harder we trudged onward, the deeper our ruts became. Some days I could actually see the ruts. These were the days I had miraculously seen or felt the goodness of God . . . then looked down at the condition of my soul, and cried, *What am I doing here? Oh, God, can't you pull me out?*

And for those who see God as an angry, ready-to-zap-you God, I can only say that though I deserved it, and though it would have been well within his rights, he didn't throw me to the lions. Instead, he proved to this hard-headed child of his that he is a Father of unending patience and unconditional love. And he did it not by might but by the quiet gentleness of his nature in the mountains of New Mexico.

[1] Jeremiah 31:33b, NAS
[2] Matthew 15:16-20, LB
[3] I Timothy 4:1-2, LB
[4] John 8:32, NAS

# PART IV

# THE HIGH ROAD

# 15

# GOD'S MYSTERIOUS WAYS

This was our fourth trip to Red River, New Mexico. It was one of our favorite places to unwind and forget the everyday grind of running our businesses. A home builder, Ronnie was not under as much pressure day-in and day-out as I was in my advertising agency, but his business was full of high-dollar risks carrying its own form of stress.

We loved the mountains, and sometimes we went to Colorado, but New Mexico was one day closer to us, and that in itself held an allure. The year before we had camped throughout the northwest, setting up our tent every evening and moving on in the morning. After three weeks, we decided tent camping was a thing of our fondly remembered, but definitely youthful, past. Still wanting to enjoy our beloved mountains, we opted for a pop-up camper. This was the trip to try it out.

Ronnie and I both loved to hike in the mountains, but my idea of hiking and his idea of hiking were literally miles apart. He could easily hike all day up and down mountains, packing gallons of water for the trip, whereas I liked those two or three mile trails on scenic paths not too far from civilization.

This was not a first marriage for either of us. One thing we had learned through past experience is the secret of lasting love lies in the art of compromise. So we decided that on this trip Ronnie would hike in the mornings while I indulged in some mental R & R, then in the afternoon we would hike, ride bikes, shop or go for a drive.

After coffee the first morning, Ronnie left for his hike. I gathered up my essentials – a chair, bottle of Evian, my Franklin Planner and favorite writing pen – and walked to a quiet spot by a running mountain stream. Here is where I was to plan my life. This was something totally alien to me, and because of that I was fighting off a growing apprehension. Trying to better organize the ad agency, we had purchased Franklin Planners – a system of date keeping and time management – for our entire staff. But before we could use the planners there was one catch. To make the system totally effective, each of us was to start by evaluating his or her life and recording our personal values. Based on these values, we were to set personal and business goals for the year, establish time frames and record our progress as time marched forward. For reasons unknown to me at the time, the thought of defining my values and setting my goals caught my imagination and appealed to me on some deeper level of consciousness.

Sensing I was in for a great deal of soul searching, I had purposely put it off until my vacation. I longed for the mountains that calm the spirit, under the pines and aspens that whisper peace to the soul.

I sat quietly in the forest, trying to get in touch with a deeper part of me. The part of me too often neglected for the urgency of the moment. Hugging my knees and staring off into autumn splendor, I pondered:

*What are my values? I spend so much of my time working – do I want to be rich? I can't believe that. Money has never been a driving force in my life. Then why do I work so hard? What am I trying to prove? I love what I do; that's part of it. And I enjoy working with my clients to the point I can't say no to them. Taking pride in doing the impossible, I relish pulling the rabbit out of the hat, yet one more time. So much of my identity is tied to what I do for a living I've lost track of who I am. If my business were gone tomorrow, who would I be?*

My mind was a jumble. The peace I'd sought from the pines, aspens and icy-blue brook eluded me. Full of questions and no answers, without one word written and no closer to achieving my task, I closed my eyes and searched into my past for clues. I looked at my watch and was startled to see both hands pointing to twelve. For five hours I had stared into the hollow of my soul. I was no closer to understanding who I was and what I wanted than before. I hoped tomorrow's dawn would break through the fog.

As I walked back to our campsite, Ronnie saw me just in time to hold a "ssh" finger to his mouth, indicating that something cute and easily scared was close by. I walked as quietly as I could over crackly autumn leaves to see Chip or Dale on hind legs begging to be fed. Tender-hearted as ever I've seen a man, Ronnie had spent the past fifteen-minutes making friends with our little neighbor. The sweetness of that moment lifted my spirits and gave me hope that all would be well.

"How was the hike? I asked, my eyes following the chipmunk's antics as he darted up the mountain.

"Good. Found a trail I'd like to try this afternoon. You game?" Ronnie looked hopeful.

"Sounds great, should clear my head. I didn't get much accomplished this morning." I left it at that.

Gathering my pack, I headed for the Jeep. But my thoughts returned to the puzzle, *Who am I?" What am I doing with my life?* All those advertising deadlines that seem to be live-or-die situations at the time, what do they really matter? My personal priorities have been shoved to the side so that I can spend twelve or fourteen hours at the office. Often too hyped to go home, I would join my cohorts for happy hour, then drive home in a blur. As I looked back on the pattern that had become my life, the sweetness I'd found moments before was crushed by a weight of sadness.

We drove several miles to the trailhead, parked the car and began our journey to what was described on the map as an easy trail to a beautiful waterfall. Somewhere we missed the two-mile trail to the waterfall and realized too late we were on our way to Lost Lake. *Apropos*, I thought. *A perfectly good work of God that got itself lost.* As the ten-mile trail became steeper and harder to climb, I suggested going back.

"We've come this far, there should be switchbacks soon," Ronnie pointed to the trail map to cheer me. The switchbacks angling left then right up the mountain weren't much better. Stopping every few minutes to catch my breath, I wondered what I was doing there.

Finally the trail leveled off and I sighed with relief. After winding our way through a thicket of brush, we entered a grove of deadness. As far as the eye could see, there was no life, only stumps and limbs of charred remains. The once stately trees that grew tall and proud, were reduced to dead clumps of burned wood. There was no green here, no new growth, only greys and black. The wind, which I hadn't noticed on the switchbacks, whistled eerily through the skeleton forest. Suddenly I felt very cold and very alone. I walked quickly to catch up to Ronnie and grabbed his hand. "This is too weird, it's giving me the spooks."

"It's just nature's way of thinning the forest," Ronnie calmly explained. "By next spring there will be new growth. Young trees will come up and it'll look a lot different."

Glad to leave the spooky forest behind, I quickened my pace to see what new surprises our mischievous path had in store for us.

The next moment my heart sank. Before us, the four-foot wide trail thinned to a foot-wide path as it curved around the near-vertical side of the mountain. I can't do this. "Ronnie I really can't do this, I'm afraid of heights."

"Don't look down," was his answer as he forged ahead.

I panicked. One misplaced step and I would be history. By this time, Ronnie was out of sight and I had two choices: try to get back without a map, or inch my way around the mountain. No choice really, I'd never make it back without the map and compass. I took my hat off, held it next to my head to block out the imagined view of me toppling down the mountain, and took the first step. My heart was pounding and the 11,000 foot elevation was making me dizzy. *Great.* As I walked one foot in front of the other, I realized the reason I couldn't see Ronnie was that the trail curved sharply around the mountain and I was approaching nothing but blue sky. *Don't panic, I can do this.* I took a deep breath, trying to find oxygen in the air. I inched my way around the curve and told myself to look out, not down. One false move and I would be dead. I made it, only to find more and more of the thin trail threading it's way precariously around the steep mountain.

I was energized to see Ronnie waiting for me a few yards ahead. *Now will be the perfect time to kill my husband,* I thought. One look at my face told him all he needed to know. "It's not nearly as bad as you're making out!" There was a challenge in his voice, and suddenly my courage was renewed. *I can do this, I am doing it!* Overly confident, I changed my gate and suddenly found myself sliding on loose gravel. My left leg slid over the side scraping the boulder that defined the sharp decline, my right arm flailed for something to hold onto; my hand found a thin trunk of a young tree growing out of the rock. I sat for a moment to catch my breath. *I'm okay* I told myself, nothing but a little scrape and hurt pride.

Finally, the trail spread out and we were in the forest again.

"Let's rest for a while. I'm hungry and exhausted," I said, already wriggling out of my pack.

"Thought we were going to eat at Lost Lake," Ronnie reminded me.

"Okay, let's just grab a snack here. I really need to rest." As I pulled out crackers, cheese and apples, Ronnie found his knife and commented about a bird that landed on a limb a few feet from us. "I wonder what kind of bird that is. He's been following us for over a mile." Whatever kind he was he was ready to share our snack, totally unthreatened by humans invading his domain. Almost coming close enough to be touched, he seemed to welcome the company. Come to think of it, this trail was deserted. We hadn't seen another human since we left the switchbacks. *Some people are just smarter than others,* I mused.

Rested and feeling like I might really live through this, I put on my pack and we hiked through the forest to a clearing. There seemed to be dozens of trails going in as many directions; some of the trail just stopped as boulders blocked the way. With many false starts and dead-ins, we eventually found our way.

The last mile seemed endless as my body trudged forward on shaky legs. The slow, steady incline was almost worse than the steep trails up the mountain. Drinking water every few minutes and breathing harder for air without any substance, I was ready to say, "Who really gives a flip what Lost Lake looks like?" and turn around. But we had come too far to give up now. Throughout the hike, Ronnie's pace had never changed, and by now I was finding it downright irritating. "Aren't you tired?" I asked.

"Not really," he answered. I vowed to never ask again.

As if knowing I needed a little push and spark of encouragement, a man and woman came bounding toward us. "Hi!" they called out in unison.

"Hey! How's the lake?" we asked.

"It's beautiful and worth the trip," the woman said as she passed. "You're almost there!"

With new energy and determination, I pushed on.

Fifteen minutes later we saw it. The top of the mountain had been scooped out, as if by God's hand, and filled with the most beautiful crystal clear water I had ever seen. The sight was awesome. We slowly and silently made our way down to the lake, proceeding almost reverently. A hymn started playing in my head and I hummed to its melody, "This is my Father's world . . . He speaks to me everywhere."[1] We stayed there only for a moment, feeling like trespassers. The beauty surreal, too pure to be defiled, this was a different world within our world. The only distraction to the idyllic scene was the force of a mighty wind blowing over the mountain and across the lake. Its power so strong we had difficulty standing against its might. Without saying a word, we slowly walked back to the trail.

Solemnly we ate our dinner, then headed back down the mountain. I was amazed at how fast we retraced our steps, making it around and down the mountain in less than two hours. Even my fear of heights seemed to be overcome as I maneuvered the thin threading trail that had been such an obstacle to me earlier.

Feeling good about my day's accomplishment, I slept soundly that night and dreamt about the kind and friendly bird that had hovered unnoticed as I walked foot over foot on the precarious trail around the steep mountain. I dreamt that my little guardian was at home in a branch of a tree overhanging Lost Lake.

At this point in my story, I wish I could write, "I understood fully the significance of my hike to Lost Lake and what God was showing me." In all honesty it took years for me to appreciate the richness of my adventure with its colorful symbolisms and divinely painted metaphors along the way. At the time, I just didn't get it. It never occurred to me that God was reaching out to me. I was convinced that as I struggled along my real life journey, he was too disgusted with me to see or care what I had done to my life.

But I was wrong.

God truly does work in mysterious ways. But you must be sensitive to feel his leading. You must be silent to hear him talking. And you must expect his presence to know that he is there. In the quietness of his nature, he was revealing to me the very thing that my heart longed to hear. While my intellect did not grasp the full significance of his message until years later, my spirit must have understood. For it was the next day after my journey to Lost Lake that my hand reached up to his and I found him eager and willing to rescue me. This simple act of faith changed my life.

The next day after driving Ronnie to a trailhead a few miles from camp, I went back to our camper and prepared myself for another morning by the mountain stream. Straddling a rock, I stared onto the page with VALUE printed across the top preceeded by a line on which I am to write the type of value. Seemingly I needed to categorize my values. Was it a family value, a business value, a personal value or a spiritual value? Under the heading, 46 lines ran horizontally across the page providing 46 thin spaces in which I was to bare my soul.

As I sat staring at the word VALUE, a melody drifted through my head and the memory of Lost Lake and its formidable trail came forward in my mind. Sensing the hike was not taken by chance, and feeling acutely the presence of God, I bowed my head and began to pray. *Oh God, help me sort things out. You know how confused I am. I need you to show me the way back to you. I willfully blunder through life, independently making decisions that are not good for me. But oh God, these things I choose don't satisfy. My life is rough terrain. I wobble on cliffs, looking out, looking down, but seldom up. I feel so empty. Lord, you have given me a sign, a sign of hope that there's still a chance for me. You have shown me the life you intended for me and I felt so uncomfortable there – like I didn't belong.*

I sat quietly for many minutes, allowing my mind to relax and feel the calm of the forest. Enveloped in a peacefulness that only God can bestow, I finally knew what I was to write.

On September 10, 1992, I wrote the words that my Father had been longing to hear: **My value is not found in myself. It is found in God and who he wants me to be.**

*But how do I find out who he wants me to be?*
*Seek out people to help me. Friends who honestly seek truth, those not religious, but struggling to understand. Those with a contrite and simple heart. Seek out a spiritual family. I need to start over. I need to concentrate on reframing all my values and beliefs – not based on anything learned in the past, traditions or religions. I need to forgive again and learn tolerance. I need to reconcile my intellect with my faith. I need to get over my anger. I need to appreciate where others are in their journey, loving them and praying for understanding. I need to withdraw the aura of superiority, which is really a feeling of inferiority. A feeling that others have found The Secret and are more worthy than I. (I know that God speaks differently to each of his children.) I need a contrite heart, a servant's heart. I need to see and admit my shortcomings, pray for forgiveness. I need to be close to God – to listen to that inner voice. I need to trust again.*

**Oh God help me to:**

•**stop trying to make you like I am. (Psalms 50: 21b: 'You thought that I was just like you.')** *I know my ways are not your ways. You are God and I am just a willful, disobedient spoiled brat.*

- **stop being afraid to ask for forgiveness because I am fearful of falling back into sin.**
- **prioritize my life. I'm too weighted down with business.**
- **stop going to happy hour and associating with people who aren't living for You.** *Give me new priorities, new friends, a new life.*
- **be a better wife to Ronnie.** *Help me to commit to him totally and trust him completely. Help me to love him unconditionally.*
- **help me to have a servant's heart, not balancing good deeds/bad deeds on the scales of love.** *But help me to be willing to give more than my share.*

As I poured my heart onto the pages of my planner, I knew that God was there and understood my sincerity. My soul's desire was to change. What I had written was not a flippant wish-list. With his help, it was what I purposed to live.

Later that evening as Ronnie and I sat by the crackling campfire, I sensed in the autumn air the freshness of a new beginning. The brilliant stars in the mountain sky illuminated the dusty road that wound through the quiet campgrounds; its reddish-brown earth would sleep peacefully till the dawn. There was not a pothole nor gremlin in sight.

[1]This is My Father's World, text by Maltbie D. Babcock, music by Franklin L. Sheppard

# 16

# RESTORING THE YEARS

For the next year, I took baby steps. God and I did not accomplish everything I had planned overnight. But I knew that my heart was changed, and somehow I understood that when the time was right, everything I asked him to do would be done.

While I was waiting, I became extremely curious about God's personality. *Who are you God?* I knew he was patient and long-suffering. Said to be a God of second chances, for me he was a God of unlimited chances. I knew without a doubt that he loved me unconditionally. The light had finally dawned. I could relate to this, because as a mother I knew there was nothing my children could do that would make me stop loving them. But there were so many things I did not know about God.

In my search for an intimate knowledge of God, I didn't expect a divine revelation or supernatural intervention on my behalf. After all, I was just a babe feeding on milk. At this point, I had no idea what to expect. In retrospect, I see the most ordinary of human contacts as divine appointments. A chance meeting here, a word there, all quite mundane in human terms, but in heavenly terms it meant lots of angel hours on my behalf!

In defining my spiritual values and goals, I had asked God for friends who would help me. People who honestly sought truth, those not religious, but **real** people struggling to understand. Those with a contrite and simple heart. I asked him to give me new priorities, new friends, a new life and a spiritual family.

When I was ready, my loving Father gave me everything I asked for and abundantly more!

It began with a simple business meeting that turned into a wonderful time of sharing between two of the Father's kids. "You go to Highland? So do I!" I said.

"You do? I've never seen you there," Stan said in surprise.

"Well, I've kept a pretty low profile over the years," I admitted. "I really like the music at Highland, so I go to worship service. But since I left the single's group, I haven't gotten involved with the people."

Stan must have caught something in my voice as he offered, "It's a pretty big church and hard to meet people if you don't belong to a small group. If you're interested in a really good Bible study, you should try my Precept Ministries Class. We're studying the Gospel of John at the 9:15 hour."

"Yeah, maybe I will," I said.

Every time we met after that, Stan and I would talk more about the Lord than the business at hand. Over the next year, we developed a friendship that God used to answer many of my prayers. I finally did join the Precept Class and begin my journey toward spiritual maturity.

The concept of inductive Bible study was different than anything I had ever experienced. This was definitely not your gloss-over-the-surface Bible study. It involved two or three hours of study a night, plus the purchase of Greek and Hebrew study books heavy enough to kill small rodents.

My first Precept class was on the last half of the book of John. Through this study I virtually lived the final days of Christ's time on earth. In his infinite wisdom, the Lord knew I needed to walk again in the steps of Jesus. I needed to feel the pain, the agony and the cost of his love for me. In every way, it was the symbolic beginning of my spiritual journey. I had begun at the cross, and after many wasted years, I had finally returned to the cross. But this time as a grown woman who understood fully the weight of sin, the power of Satan and the price Jesus had to pay for my redemption.

There are no words to describe the aching in my heart when we studied the torture Jesus suffered at the hands of the Roman soldiers. All my life, I thought the crucifixion was the greatest assault against Christ. Now I was learning the true nature of the crimes against Jesus. I understood for the first time what scourging meant. I saw skin hanging like ribbons from his body, his insides revealed. His head not just bloodied with thorns, but with open holes in his skull. And with barely the energy to stand, much less the ability to walk, he was made to carry his own cross to Golgotha's Hill. And during his long walk and his three hours on the cross, people laughed, spat, called him names, gambled for his clothing, gave him vinegar to drink and finally gouged him with a spear. The actual scene that day at Calvary is far different than any artist's rendition of the crucifixion, with Jesus hanging, head bowed to one side, a few streams of blood running down his body. The reality would be too horrid to bear.

Never again will Good Friday be a waste of a sunny afternoon. Never again will Easter be a new dress in my closet. The cross has wrought a miraculous healing in me and the resurrection a new life.

I had finally found the journey map.

It was my Bible.

It had been there all along, gathering dust on a bookshelf.

Suddenly alive and full of infinite power, it became my constant companion and source of change.

People started noticing changes in me immediately. I stopped socializing with friends who didn't help me in my search to know God. It wasn't that I didn't like them any more – I simply did not have time. My time was extremely valuable now. I had wasted more than enough time, thank you very much. But I was not lonely. In his graciousness, he replaced those friends with sisters and brothers who to this day, hold me accountable, encourage me in my walk and struggle along with me when I fail.

The biggest ache in my heart was the time I had wasted living for myself. I had lost the first bloom of love experienced in my early years as a Christian. Those years were gone. I could not get them back – or could I? Studying one day, I came upon a verse that said, "I will restore the years."[1] I read it again. Then I read all around it to make sure I was not taking it out of context. Wow! *You can do that too, Lord?* Amazing. I had not thought of that. Now that I knew it was possible, I claimed it. *God, you said you will restore the years, and now I'm trusting you to do it.*

The way he did it came as a surprise (surprise, surprise).

I had subscribed to a Christian tape-of-the-month some months before. Their quarterly newsletter was sent to me and as I breezed through it, an announcement jumped off the page. Successful Christian Living Ministries was inviting me to go to Israel. *Israel?* I guess I am one of the few Christians alive who never wanted to go to Israel. I thought of Israel as a very dangerous place with sand and hot sun. *Israel? Why Israel, why not Switzerland or England?*

But I knew – without a shadow of doubt I knew. I was so excited about going, it was unnatural. I did not know what the Lord had in store for me, but I was ready nonetheless. My mom went with me and together we trekked to the unknown. There were thirty-two people from ten states in our group. Married and single, young and old; in ten short days these strangers became a family who shared a life-changing experience.

At dawn on our third day in Israel, I went out on the hotel deck overlooking the calm, blue Sea of Galilee and prepared for this important day. I was to be baptized in the Jordan River, the same river in which John the Baptist had baptized Jesus so many years ago. I sat quietly meditating on a verse that had become extremely important to me . . . "I beseech you therefore brethren, by the mercies of God, that ye present your bodies a living sacrifice, holy, acceptable unto God, which is your reasonable service."[2] For me, this verse meant total submission to God. It meant making Jesus Lord of my life, which I had finally done. I was now coming to him as an obedient child, trusting him with my life. It had taken me too many years, but I was finally his and this baptism was the symbolic beginning to the next stage of my journey.

The whole of Israel was too overwhelming to ever

describe accurately. Like the twelve disciples, we walked, ate, laughed, cried, learned – and grew to love one another. We rode together on a wooden fishing boat across the Sea of Galilee, and we sat overlooking the Mount of Beatitudes. We joined with a group of hundreds in singing an extemporaneous "How Great Thou Art" in the Church of Ann, sang praise songs in the Upper Room, and celebrated communion in the garden where Jesus is reported to have been buried. We walked the streets of Bethlehem and Jerusalem, and we toured the wilderness.

And each night I lay in my bed pouring over my Bible, learning more about David, Saul, Samson, Abraham, Deborah, Rachel and Moses. Characters I had heard about as a child in Sunday School and Vacation Bible School were suddenly becoming quite real to me. The places where their stories unfolded leaped off of the thin parchment and became rocks, caves, creek beds, mountains and brightly arrayed valleys.

When I returned home, I was so full of the experience my husband perceptively said, "You have so much inside, it will be hard for you to concentrate until you communicate it all." He was right. But it was not until a few weeks later that I fully understood what the Lord was wanting to communicate to *me*. It was another hiking trip that indirectly led me to my next spiritual plateau.

Trying to be a good wife, I agreed to backpack with Ronnie in Big Bend National Park. If climbing a mountain with a 25-pound pack in 90 degree heat is not a labor of love, I don't know what is. The only thing that got me up that mountain was the thought of coming down. (I had learned the exhilaration of coming *down* the mountain on the trail from Lost Lake.)

We finally made it to our camp site which turned out to be a patch of grass beside some scrubs. Knowing that we were the only campers in the area, and that bears had been sited in the park, did not help me sleep any better that night. The next day we hiked for ten hours, through breathtaking scenery, to find the only natural water source in the dry, primitive area. Siphoning slimy-green water from an almost empty hole in a rock, we filtered it through charcoal until it was clear. Well, almost. Its saving grace was that it was wet and would keep us from dehydration.

Packing gallons of "wet stuff" back to our camp, I collapsed into a funny little chair that sat inches from the ground, took off my hiking boots and put on my sandals. Ronnie, still full of energy, heated coffee on something that looked like a blow torch with a cup suspended over its flame. In minutes, the water was blistering and did just that as the cup tipped over, spewing the boiling liquid over my left foot and toes. The incredible pain of what would turn out to be second degree burns made me forget everything I learned as a Girl Scout. I immediately cried out to Ronnie, "Hurry, I need butter!" (my grandma's home remedy for burns) Thinking on his feet, Ronnie ran for our precious water as I screamed, "Don't waste the water." He ignored me, pouring the soothing cool liquid over my burns. I cried, moaned and groaned but there was nothing more we could do. Knowing that packing down the mountain in the dark was not an option, I painfully prepared for a long night.

At dawn Ronnie broke camp and loaded most of the weight from my backpack into his. After he doctored my foot with Second Skin and wrapped it, the new dilemma was how to get all of that into my hiking boot.

Fortunately my boot had a wide tongue and long shoes laces, so we managed without too much damage to my injury. Limping down the mountain, using a stick Ronnie had prepared for my descent, took hours longer than it would have under normal conditions.

Leaving Big Bend Park with our mountain in the rear view mirror, we knew we had not seen all we came to see, but we had an adventure that we will never forget.

In my life before Lost Lake, being confined to bed for ten days with a burned foot would have seemed like the end of the world. I would have been on the phone with the office every few minutes, working on my Powerbook computer and faxing frantically. My new life was different, and I made wise use of my time. Ever since Israel I'd had a voracious appetite for God's Word. I wanted to know everything. Chapters and verses I knew I had skimmed over before took on new meaning. With Israel clear in my mind's eye, I would think *Hey, I've been there. I saw that. It's a real place!* I began reading in Genesis and grudgingly limped back to work after finishing 2 Kings. I had the most wonderful time. It was not the first time I had read these first fourteen books of the Bible, but this time was different. Before, the Old Testament was full of weird sounding places such as Enghedi, and the people seemed like wooden characters from old world fables. Now these weird-sounding places had texture and depth and on the people I saw flesh and facial features; they had feelings and desires, pain and joy. Their experiences were as real to me as my own, and in those intense days of learning God's Word, I knew that I was in an accelerated class at the feet of the Master Teacher.

God showed me how I, like the Israelites, had wandered in the desert for many years. And as he had stayed with them – a cloud by day and a fire by night – I knew he had never been far from me. Even as they had turned away, seeking after other gods, I too had worshipped the things on earth rather than him. Yet, he said to them thousands of years ago, as he said to me that day, "I will be with you; I will not fail you or forsake you."[3] Who can understand such love?

During the time I was recuperating, I also learned more of his personality. Through the Holy Spirit, he showed me that I had lost sight of the God of the trinity. I could love and relate to Jesus as my Savior and now my Lord. I was beginning to appreciate the workings of the Holy Spirit, but I had lost my fear of my Father, God. I eagerly called Him "Abba" (Daddy) and related to him in terms of love, forgiveness and understanding. But now I realized I had missed the magnitude of who he is and what he is. Maybe I was a little scared to think of the wonder of his glory and the depth of his passion. While writers through the ages have portrayed man's quest for God, throughout Scripture, the reality is that it is *God* who seeks after *man*. It is God who steps into our history and his *own* will which he seeks.

And more than anything else I learned that the most significant thing I could do with my life was to spend time alone with God. At the end of those two weeks of meditation, prayer and study, I felt refreshed and more spir-itually alive than I had in over twenty years. God had been faithful in answering all my prayers. He had restored the years. I felt the closeness to him I had felt when I was first saved; but now the intimacy bore deeper and proved rich-er. He and I had been through a lot. He knew I had learned a lesson I would never forget, and I knew he was a God I could trust with my life.

For years following my trip to Lost Lake, I looked back on my value list to make sure there was nothing left for God and I to do. Eventually, I had the eerie sense that he had taken a copy of it and checked things off as he gave me the strength and will to accomplish each goal. Since then he has shown me new things I need to achieve and places in my heart that need to change. I have learned it is an ongoing process that will never stop. The closer I draw near to him, the more imperfections I see in me.

You may be wondering if it was hard to break free of all that junk in my life. I discovered one thing that might help you. I believe that in every prodigal's life there is a stumbling sin. It is the temptation that caused you to fall into your pothole. Once you free yourself from your stumbling sin, many of the others disappear. At least, that is what I found in my life. For me, it was drinking. I was not an alcoholic. I drank socially. Unfortunately in my profession, there seemed to be far too many social occasions. And when you drink, you are naturally friends with people who like to drink and party. But the worst part was alcohol freed all my inhibitions. I did things while drinking that I would never dream of doing while sober. I also wasted time. I got into a habit of going to happy hour with people from my office almost every night. Intending to unwind with only one drink, the next thing I knew the night was shot. At least one day a week, I was so hung-over that only a Big Mac for breakfast would get me to the office. And of course, one cannot sit in a smoky bar without smoking.

One morning I woke up and said aloud, "Okay,

God. I will quit today." I had no idea *why* I said that, but I knew what it meant. My spirit must have been communing with God in my sleep. That day I quit smoking and I quit drinking. No, it was not hard to quit drinking. Yes, it was hard to quit smoking. So hard I started chewing Nicorette Gum and these many years later am still chewing Nicorette Gum! But I have not had a cigarette, and I am thankful for that.

If you are serious about changing your life, search out that stumbling sin. It might be the most pleasurable thing you do and the last thing you want to give up. But until you show God you are serious, you will never be free. I can promise you when he knows you are serious about change, he will make it easier than you ever dreamed possible.

He has a way of drawing new interests into your life. What you once thought was fun and exciting will suddenly make you gag. And before you know it, you will find new people appearing in your space. Pay close attention because angels are in your midst. From the moment you and God get serious, nothing will happen by chance. Watch for the miracles, they will be happening daily. You probably won't recognize them for a while, but after you're in tune with your spirit, these everyday miracles become quite obvious.

I could go on and on about what God wants to do in your life. I know because I've experienced his blessings first hand. But first you must hear the truth. The absolute, number one, most important, paramount truth I can tell you.

There is only one way to positively stay on the road God planned for your life.
There is only one way to stay free.

There is only one way to resist temptation.

There is only one way to walk in Christ's footsteps.

There is only one way to stay in complete fellowship with God.

There is only one way to abide in Jesus.

There is only one way to renew your spirit and transform your mind.

There are no miracle potions and no short cuts. The only way to knock Satan clean off his high-horse so that you can stay on the high road is found in your journey map – God's Word.

[1] Joel 2:25a, author's paraphrase

[2] Romans 12:1-2, KJ

[3] Joshua 1:5b, NAS

# 17

# THE JOURNEY MAP

Reading books about God, listening to teaching tapes, sitting in church, hearing God's Word, all of these are extremely helpful and good ideas for a Christian. But I've learned that nothing will ground you to the Rock like studying his Word. It is not enough to just read it. Prayerfully study it. Dig into it. Study the words. Find the answers on your own by letting scripture interpret scripture. I have found this kind of study in the Precept courses by Kay Arthur. And would highly recommend that you search out a course offered in your area. I can guarantee that if you are serious about wanting to break free, this is the way to do it. Even those who thought they knew the Bible are humbled to see new truths come alive through inductive study.

I fear many of us who do not go to the Bible to search for answers "lean on our own understanding,"[1] thinking highly of our advanced state of intellectualism. How prideful and foolish we appear to God.

I lived so much of my life thinking that whatever I thought was right for me, whatever Joe thought was right for him, whatever Ann thought was right for her. I prided myself on my tolerance toward others' beliefs. It never occurred to me that there could be real right and wrong answers.

I've always had a difficult time accepting the concept of absolute truths. As a writer for my advertising agency, I've been trained to look for many right answers in finding solutions to marketing problems. I have always been able to see multiple sides to every situation. My mind doesn't work like an accountant's mind, digging and searching for that one absolute answer that is the sum and total of my work for that day. Consequently, through much of my life I've been "tossed here and there by waves, and carried about by every wind of doctrine."[2] Without any absolute truths to hold onto, I believed in whatever seemed right for me. Proverbs has a verse about people like me: "He who separates himself (from God) seeks his own desire. He quarrels against all sound wisdom. A fool does not delight in understanding, but only in revealing his own mind."[3] I think that could apply to many of us; we delight in revealing our own minds without any thought of what God said about it, without any thought of whether it is right or wrong. As long as we think it's right, it must be.

Those with black and white, disciplined minds have a much easier time of it, than those of us with colorful, adventurous minds. I envy my friends who see truth immediately without having to go through the "what if" exercises that are so time consuming for me.

There was a time when I couldn't see the Bible's relevancy for modern man. In my unbelief, I wondered where God was. Couldn't he do something about this world's spinning out of control? Did he just leave us here to fend for ourselves against corrupt politicians, drunken drivers, murderers, rapists? Thinking how he intervened for his children throughout the Bible, I thought, *Where have you been for 2,000 years? Why are you so silent? Aren't we just as important to you as someone like Lot for goodness sake?* In my infinite wisdom, I decided that God must have formed the world, set up "Mother Nature" to rule the elements, created man and then let it rip to see what would happen. Seeing that it wasn't going too well, I envisioned him returning to his management position over the angels in heaven. From time to time he'd look down, sigh and turn his back for another few years, hoping that we'd come to our senses.

It was in my Precept study of the book of Daniel that I finally, without a doubt understood the foundation of my faith and the answers to my questions. The overriding theme of this prophetic work is "God is in control." Not only is he keenly aware of what is going on in every believer's life, he chooses the leaders of nations for his purposes and he's responsible for the rise and fall of empires from ancient times through today. There is a grand scheme to all that happens, and nothing happens without his foreknowledge. Mentally comprehending this is one thing, but understanding the magnitude of this truth in your heart is another. There is order to the universe that God created. Order to the mysterious happenstances of life.

As you learn to trust God with your life, you understand more and more that whatever happens is according to his will. Yes, he sometimes allows bad things to happen.

A child dies.

Divorce ravages a family.

A single mom is diagnosed with cancer.

And we wonder why.

Just as Job's friends wondered at the calamities that overtook such a godly man, humans throughout the ages have asked the question, "Why?" There is no pat answer, but I have found in my life that all things truly have worked out for the best. Even heartache, when handled with care, can leave a sweet aroma as you walk through it in faith coming out on the other side a deeper, richer, more compassionate person. I believe the key is perspective.

Could it be that my life on earth is a training ground for heaven? While I am consumed with the ticking of the clock and the stretching of my days, God sees my time here as a "vapor of steam"[4]? I believe this. The Bible teaches it. I now understand that the importance lies not so much in what happens to me here on earth, but in how I respond to what happens. I have come to understand that the trials and tribulations of my life shored up my strength and reinforced the fabric of my character.

God understood that many a doubting Thomas would need tangible proof that the Bible is inspired and not written by man. In the book of Daniel, written during his life from 605 B.C to 536 B.C., an understanding and loving God revealed exactly what would happen throughout the ages until the end times. History bears witness to the accuracy of these prophecies. 2,500 years of prophecy is now history. What remains to be experienced are the final days, those times yet to come. Here we read of the antichrist who will deceive the world into believing he is a peaceful and just leader, only to bring about human entrapment and final destruction. But this too is part of God's plan and will usher in the second coming of Christ and his reign on earth.

As a child my grandma made sure I knew about Bible prophecy. I can still see her bent over the well-worn pages, a magnifying glass over the words she was reading to me. Her face became animated as she told me about Israel's finally becoming a nation. This was the beginning, she said, the fig tree was blooming. With admonishments to watch carefully the events that took place in this tiny country because they would signal the fulfillment of Biblical prophecy, she felt excitement in seeing the beginning of the end. But in her voice there was also dread for what lay ahead. She told me about the antichrist and what to expect when the end time was drawing near, things I could hardly believe at the time. "Times will be so bad," she said, "you won't be able to walk in your neighborhood at night. Your children will not be safe. Families will fight and kill each other. At the very end, no one will be able to work or buy food without the mark of the beast (antichrist.) Christians who stand in their faith will not survive."

Talk about scaring an eight-year-old! But then I thought, how can this be? Living in the 50s without a care in the world, we never locked our doors and we walked in the dark without a worry. At this young age, I even rode the bus to downtown St. Louis with my ten-year-old cousin for an afternoon shopping trip. It seemed impossible that the world could deteriorate so fast. And what was the mark of this beast thing? It was thirty years later that I understood how quickly computers and credit cards had provided the way for each person to be "marked" for destruction.

And as we move closer to a new world order and a global economy, we are organizing our world in a neat little bundle, prepared especially for the first and last world leader, the antichrist. We may not be able to read the end of the story in our history books, but we have something even more chilling . . . reality. We are living the end-time prophecy.

The Bible is complete because God is the Alpha and Omega, the beginning and the end. He has given his children a book with road maps to follow. A love letter to those who believe, a terrifying, impossible-to-understand collection of words to the unbelieving.

I have always found it puzzling that intelligent people who usually have all their facts straight in anything relating to worldly wisdom, will scoff at the Bible. When asked if they have ever read it, the answer is inevitably no. They will say it is written by man, which truly shows they know nothing of the depth of the writings. What other book has withstood the test of time, has been analyzed by so many scholars, can be read hundreds of times and still not fully understood? What other book has the power to give life? Change a life? And remains an enigma without the supernatural revelation by the Holy Spirit?

I am convinced that studying the Word and regularly taking time to be alone with God is the only way a Christian can live the abundant life our creator intended.

In Jim Bakker's book, *I Was Wrong*, he confesses that while preaching God's Word, he really didn't know it. He chose verses here and verses there to build the prosperity doctrine exalted by his TV show and embraced by its audience. In prison, he began to study the scriptures for the first time. He painstakingly explored the meanings of the words in the original Greek and Hebrew languages until he finally understood that what he had preached to millions of people did not line up with the Word of God. He was horrified. He had deceived his followers and was crushed with the immensity of his mistake.

Yes, Jim Bakker was wrong, but what of the millions of followers who sat by their television screens being spoon fed a lie? What was their responsibility? Had they dug into the Word and known the truth, would they have been deceived? Not hardly. They would have turned their sets off and tied up their purse strings.

We cannot go on expecting every silver-tongued televangelist to speak the truth. Nor can we totally rely on our pastor's Sunday morning sermon to propel us past Wednesday. It is every believer's responsibility to seek out truth. It is every believer's responsibility to discern God's will for his life. And the only way to do that is to spend time in prayer, study and meditation.

*Whoa! You say, this sounds too much like work.* It may *sound* like work, but I can tell you, I've never had so much fun in my life. Ever. God has given me an unquenchable thirst for his knowledge. The more I learn, the more I crave to learn. There is nothing more fascinating than to read a scripture that makes you go, "Huh?" And then all of a sudden go, "Ah-Ha!" Where does this enlightenment come from?

Remember when Jesus was consoling his disciples, telling them a Helper would come? He said the Helper would be a Spirit that would lead them to truth. Can you imagine? *What in the world are you talking about, Jesus? A spirit? You're going away and leaving us with a ghost?* Sounds pretty spooky, right? But it didn't take them long to understand that this was no ordinary Casper. This Spirit had BIG-TIME POWER. The kind of power that turned Peter from a wuss to a wonder.

Have you ever tried to imagine how the disciples and early Christians reacted to being filled with this new power? One minute they were sober, the next minute people actually thought they were drunk. I guess these power agents finally got used to it, because throughout the book of Acts they performed miracles just like it was old hat. Then many of them sat down to write. The Bible says that the Spirit inspired their writings as they recalled the teachings and life of Jesus. And then God breathed life into every word.

So it's no wonder that it's the Holy Spirit's job to teach. He inspired the Book. He was sent here to be our helper, our teacher and our guide. If you've ever tried to read the Bible without his help, I'm sure you became frustrated. You simply can't do it without his help. He will turn a huh? into an ah-ha! if you ask him. But so many people try to read the Bible like a novel. From Page One to The End. I've heard people say, "I couldn't get past the begets." Well, who could? They are not very interesting until you understand their importance.

Try reading the Gospel of John first. It is relatively easy reading and tells an intriguing story with a plot, a climax and grand finale. John was a great friend to Jesus and his heart comes through every word he recorded.

And don't be afraid of your Bible. Even though the words are sacred, the book is your friend. If you are in the market to buy a new Bible, I would highly recommend The Inductive Study Bible, New American Standard. When you read something significant, don't be afraid to highlight it or underline it. Make notes in the wide margins – that's why they're there. In short, have fun. God doesn't want us to worship the book, he wants us to worship the author!

Now that I have told you the most important truth you will ever need to sustain your new life, there's one other item that might need your attention. Your life will change and those around you will marvel. But what of the hurts that you have inflicted on those close-by? Your loved ones who saw your testimony go glub-glub down the toilet.

[1]Proverbs 3:5b, Author's paraphrase
[2]Ephesians 4:14b, NAS
[3]Proverbs 18:1-2, NAS
[4]James 4:14, author's paraphrase

# 18

# FACING THE DRAGON

I've learned that even though the Father fully forgives and brings restoration to his children, there are consequences to pay for careless actions. The hurts I inflicted on others didn't magically go away. But God was gracious, and he provided the wisdom, strength and courage to go forward.

Sitting between my mother and my daughter on a plane to Greenville, South Carolina, I was beaming. It was a weekend any mother would eagerly anticipate. Parrish was graduating from Bob Jones University, and soon I would see my son and his little family. While he was in school, we'd eventually grown accustomed to long separations, but since my granddaughter's birth in September, I'd counted the days between visits. We hadn't been together since Christmas and I anticipated a glorious family reunion.

It had been an idyllic day with the graduation ceremony in the morning, tourist sites during the afternoon and now an Italian restaurant. The evening began as usual with our collected observations of the waiter's expertise. This was a matter of great debate as Parrish, a waiter throughout his last two years of college, had definite ideas on the subject. Generally more critical about food service than the rest of the family, he pointed out nuances that were completely beyond *our* expectations. The lighthearted banter continued until something my daughter said sent up a warning signal in my soul. I knew the evening was in trouble. It was not so much what she said, but the edge in her voice that brought me to attention. In an instant, the conversation turned from the meaningless chatter which made for easy digestion of Italian cuisine to a multi-layered dialogue of family relationships, ours in particular. *Oh, no. Not now, Jayne. We're leaving tomorrow. Can't we just have this one night without conflict?* But that wasn't to be.

My two children, born thirteen months apart, are as different as night and day. Jayne, always the "little mother," was born with responsibility engraved on her heart. With an uncanny ability to remember every detail, she was the one who made sure I remembered the dental appointment on Tuesday or the parent-teacher meeting on Thursday night. Parrish, always the class clown and always in some kind of "boys-will-be-boys" trouble, was the absent minded professor in the making.

Parrish was only one year old when his dad and I divorced. When my children's two divergent personalities became apparent, I depended upon Jayne to watch over her younger brother. They were extremely close and loving as children, but now they live separate lives with more than miles to keep them apart. The intensity of their pain, wrought through shared memories of divorces, remarriages, abusive step-parents and lost childhood, sharpens as they interact. One mis-spoken word brings an onslaught of angry words and tears. Borne out of hurt and deep-seated resentment that neither of them can understand nor come to terms with, these feelings hang in the air like a threatening storm. I have come to understand that the choices I have made in my life have much to do with the confusion in their relationship, and it breaks my heart.

Parrish and I have always been able to honestly vent our emotions. But Jayne's guarded feelings lay on the surface of her heart, filtering words and disappointments through shadows of self doubt. Knowing this has caused me to tiptoe softly through our relationship.

"Mom . . ." Jayne's calmly controlled voice brought me out of the past. "I've been working through some problems, things from my childhood that I just don't understand, and I'm having a hard time dealing with them."

*No, I screamed in my soul. I don't want to hear it. Not tonight – not ever. I want to believe that you're okay, that everything's okay. Sure your dad and I made some mistakes, what parent hasn't, but I did the best I could, didn't I?*

Not wanting to have a major family discussion in a public place surrounded by strangers, I looked for an out. On cue, my granddaughter Grace began squirming in her high chair. Relieved to find a legitimate reason to excuse myself, I rescued Grace from the confining chair, lifted her into her stroller and together we explored the shopping center which surrounded the restaurant. I couldn't have felt lower. Even her sweet little baby sounds and unconditional love did nothing to raise my spirits. My conflicting feelings were unsettling. I blamed Jayne for spoiling my dinner and myself for spoiling her life.

When my family was through eating, they came out

to join me. Acting as though nothing had happened, we drove home to my son's duplex and pretended that this was a functional family celebrating the events of the day. The evening was strained. Silent. Lost.

Unable to sleep, I stared out into the darkened room, wondering what to do for my hurting child. Somewhere around midnight, I heard her sniffles and knew she was crying. I ventured a "What's wrong, honey?" and the floodgates broke. She sobbed and I held her until she was ready to talk.

"Mom, I know I've made a lot of mistakes in my life, but don't you think you did *anything* wrong? Our family is so messed up, and you go on like everything's fine. Parrish and I can't even talk without feeling so frustrated we end up screaming at each other."

Then it was my turn to cry. And to think. *What was she saying? What did she long to hear?* Then I knew. "Oh Jayne, my darling Jayne, I would give my life to change things if I could. You have no idea how sorry I am for all the terrible choices I've made in my life. The choices I made seemed right at the time. Now I know how selfishly wrong they were and how they hurt you and your brother. I just don't know how to undo the damage."

We talked into the night about things she remembered – things I had thought, or rather hoped, were long forgotten. I tried to be as honest as I could about the motivations for my actions. They all seemed ridiculously weak in light of the damage my actions caused two of the most important people in my life, my children.

That night, though horribly painful, was a gift from the Lord. It was the first time Jayne and I had been brutally honest with each other. She had been hurt and had felt it in the workings of her life, with pain and confusion living its way out in her relationships and self-image. Loving me and fearful of confrontation, she had bottled the resentment, until finally, at the age of twenty-seven, she was able to face the dragon.

The dragon, of course, did not want to face the reality of my life – that my choices had not only hurt me but had deeply wounded my children. I wanted to believe that my kids were as resilient as I was led to believe in the books and articles I had read on why parents should get a divorce if they're not getting along. I wanted to believe that because I loved them so much in my heart, they were insulated from all the things I did in my life. The truth crashed down on top of me with a weight that I could never have borne alone. But in God's grace, my daughter and I walked through it hand-in-hand, and I learned once again that "the truth shall make you free."[1]

Jayne and I turned a corner in our relationship that night. We continue to understand that the baggage from the past has been opened, picked through and sorted out. And while still a part of our lives, its heavy weight is no longer a burden and its content is understood and no longer feared.

I encourage all prodigals to be honest with their loved ones. While I glossed over what I had done, my children grew up not understanding that their problems were my fault. They blamed themselves. They did not understand that it was not their fault. Even after I had returned to the Lord, I did not go to my kids and ask for their forgiveness. Not until I was forced to. We can't change the past, but we can accept the responsibility of our actions. And we can say, "I'm sorry.

Please forgive me. What I did was selfish and wrong." And
we can start over.

¹John 8:32, NAS

# 19

# HELPING EACH OTHER ON THE JOURNEY

Many months ago, I attended a civic meeting and found myself in the company of a group of friends from my church. As the business meeting was winding down and the refreshments were being served, a woman sitting next to me made a comment about a time in her life when she was involved in the New Age movement. Naively I asked her if this was before or after she had been saved. "Oh dear, **before** of course! Never, ever **after**." she replied. I realized my error and quickly changed the subject. But then you'll have to pardon me because I *do* know a Christian who *did* get involved in New Age *after* she had accepted Christ.

Driving home, I was bothered by this conversation. I was truly happy that this lady's experience was prior to her conversion but I wondered, by her reaction, if she would have told any of us if it had not been. "Pass the cookies please. Oh, by the way, did you know that just two short weeks ago I called my astrologist and told her I wouldn't need her any longer? And just last week I stopped channeling and stroking my crystals at night?" No, I don't think so.

Most Christians freely admit and talk at length about their sins prior to salvation. But suddenly mums the word after they've walked the aisle. Am I any different? No siree Bob. I didn't confess all because I was ashamed and fearful that others would judge me. I have even caught myself critically judging someone who was doing exactly the same thing I myself once did. Instead of expressing compassion and love, I felt holier-than-thou because I had come through it and was now beyond. I have to tell you, I think this kind of attitude makes God want to puke.

It is always a joy to meet Christians who are totally honest, those who will share their shortcomings as well as their victories. But I have found that the "bigger" the sin, the less likely they are to share. Maybe they instinctively know that they should keep their mouths shut. After all, Christians have been known to shoot their wounded. Instead of reaching out in forgiveness and understanding, many times they "tsk-tsk" and throw the guilty out into the world to fend for themselves. Not all Christians are like this. I am blessed with many friends to whom I could go to with any problem, without feeling rejected or condemned.

But I'm concerned that many Christians are afraid to drop their guard with each other at the point and time in their lives when they need comfort, reassurance and love the most. Believers hide their sins, afraid that someone will find out who they really are. If they allow the sins to become strongholds, eventually they feel too guilty to fellowship. Those who continue going to church while leading a double life have learned to separate friends and activities into experiential compartments.

I have a single friend who told me she lived like this for years. She had become so desensitized to the Spirit's tugs at her soul that she was able to do drugs and have sex on Saturday night and on Sunday take a leadership role in her church. While she believed murder was the ultimate sin, she had three abortions in two years. She confessed that while leading this double life, she was extremely critical of others, hiding her deceit behind false piety. It took a crash to the bottom and miles of road burn for her to see that she'd deceived only herself.

We need to see ourselves and each other as Christ sees us. He understands human frailty. Jesus, more than anyone else we could go to for comfort, understands the difficulty we experience in trying to live a godly life in a godless world. He understands because he became man and walked among us. And now he is our high priest sitting at the right hand of God, petitioning for us to his Father. "For we do not have a high priest who cannot sympathize with our weaknesses, but one who has been tempted in all things as we are, yet without sin."[1]

If God, who sees into the depth of our being, can love and forgive us, why can't we accept and forgive ourselves and each other? And why can't we openly communicate our hurts, our needs and our weaknesses? Speaking from experience, many times I was not able to do this because I felt overpowered. I knew there was no sense in crying my heart out to someone on Sunday, while continuing in sin during the week. Too often, I felt powerless to affect change in my life. Leaving church . . . I felt alone. Ashamed. Depressed.

It is difficult to know how to comfort people who are going through overpowering situations. What should

Christians do at this point? How do you show love to the sinner while hating the sin? I know from my own life, the "sinner" does not expect other Christians to condone what they are doing, but he does need and expect love and understanding. He needs to know that his family loves him unconditionally and will be there when he come to his senses. And the most important way a family or friend can help is to pray for the prodigal's return and full restoration. I thank God for all those who prayed me back into his arms.

I mentioned before that I have friends I could go to with any problem. These are people who have stumbled down the detour road, fallen and crawled their way out of the pothole. I have other Christian friends who wouldn't know what to do with me if I bared my soul. They are the ones whose worst nightmare is hearing themselves utter a swear word after being hit in the head with a hammer. I love both sets of friends, but choose wisely between those who can comfort and those who cannot.

We are to comfort each other in the same way God comforts us. Did God turn his back on me? No. Did he set me down and shake his finger in my face? No. What did he do that brought me out of the cold and into his arms? He drew me away from the chill by his love, then wrapped my aching soul in his blanket of compassion. This awesome encounter brought with it a formidable responsibility. We are to comfort each other in the same way God comforts us.

When prodigals return to God and seek help from other Christians, the last thing they need is a sermon on past sins. Nor do they need to feel that they are surrounded by super-spiritual wimps, who cringe at their problems. Once they are repentant and forgiven by God, they need compassion, love and help as they begin again.

Church should be the one place you can go and get any help you need, but we're really not set up that way. I think one of the problems is that long-time members are so happy to see one another and catch up with the week's news each Sunday that we don't even notice people in need or those alone and unloved. We don't intentionally neglect, but the outcome is the same. We depend on the overworked pastor to "take care of the problem people."

Many, many years ago I was going through some terrible problems. I literally had to force myself out the door, into my car and through the church doors. Sitting in my Sunday School class, I was so close to tears and so desperately in need of someone saying, "Are you okay? Can I help?" that I was sure my face was a dead give-away.

A peppy little homemaker with an exaggerated southern drawl started the class with "Isn't God sooooo special? Didn't we have such a joyful week? Won't it be soooo special to praise him today?"

I wanted to stand up and shout, "No, I had a horrible week. I didn't feel God this week. I don't even know if he cares about me. And no, I don't feel soooo anything, except scared, depressed and now a little bit angry."

Of course, I didn't say any of these things, I bit my upper lip, stifled a sob and turned to page 23 in my songbook. By the end of the class, I had repositioned my happy face and was acceptably masked to walk the church corridors greeting others as they greeted me.

A friend and I decided that every church should have a little "hospital wing" where hurting people could go and bare their souls with someone they could trust to listen without condemnation. But I doubt that many of us would drop our guard long enough to become that vulnerable with each other.

Somewhere along the line, I ditched that silly little mask and learned that I should never play poker because every emotion I feel crosses my face. On a Sunday morning not too long ago, my face must have been in a mess because a friend said, "What's wrong? Can I help?" That was all it took for me to break down and sob, telling him the hurts of my heart. It was such a freeing experience, and in that moment I made a friend for life. I thought, why haven't I done this before? And the answer came like a slap across the face: PRIDE. Just when I thought I had that puppy whipped, it bit me in the backside.

I'm not discouraged because I know my new life is an ongoing process. The potter's not finished with this lump of clay. Sometimes he molds me gently, other times he pats me hard enough to hurt. The important thing is through his grace, I have become pliable, allowing him to smooth out the rough spots of my life. I am forever grateful that when the potter saw who I was he could also see whose I would become.

[1]Hebrews 4:15, NAS

# 20

# JOURNEY'S END

Do people really hear God speak to them? Honestly, now. . . do you look for other delusional traits from people who claim that God actually spoke to *them*? Or do you write them off as kooks? Well, no wonder. We've all seen our share of mentally challenged prophets of doom running around half-naked in the streets. Enough murderous butchers who told the world that they were only carrying out God's diabolical schemes. Why should we believe anyone who says, "I heard God say . . . ?"

So when I tell you "I heard God say", I run the risk of being written off as a kook. But I'm telling you as honestly as I know how to tell you, that I heard God say twelve words as I wrote this book. I heard him say, "Tell them I love them. Tell them *how much* I love them." These twelve words did not boom from heaven like the rush of a mighty wind, but rather they quietly whispered through my thoughts. They penetrated deep into my mind until I knew the message I was to deliver. "Tell them I love them. Tell them *how much* I love them."

When I completed the previous chapters I felt confident that the Father's message had been delivered. In pondering what to say in the final chapter, I sensed a subtle shift. While the message remained the same, I recognized an urgency that I had not been conscious of before. I shut off my computer and waited. *What is it Lord? What do you want me to say?* I waited. And waited. And finally I heard my instructions. Said in four short, fearsome words, "Time is running out."

I have to tell you, I am much more comfortable delivering a message of love than one of fear. So I waited. I went back to my life. I read a couple of books, shopped, spent time with my neglected husband and studied my journey map. I even cleaned out my writing room, filing all my research notes and returning my study aids to their shelves. But even as I dawdled, the words kept coming . . . "time is running out." And so tonight I approach you with love in my heart and deep concern for the time we have remaining. My friends, it's running out.

I guess my greatest fear is that you will read this book and see how God through the ages has forgiven his wayward ne'er-do-wells and think, "That's cool. But I've got one more stumble left in me before I giddy-up to the high road." If that's the case, I can't imagine how you are going to feel when you come eyeball-to-eyeball with the God-man who willingly spread his arms, opened his hands and accepted the nails. Is one more stumble worth the shame, the regret and the humiliation?

I've sometimes wondered about the people in Noah's time. We know they laughed at Noah and his family during the time they were building the ark and rounding up their pets. And God waited 150 years before bringing the floods. I wonder if there wasn't just one person who thought, "At the first sprinkle, I'm in the boat." Maybe the guys swigging java at the Sit-A-Spell Diner taunted each other as to who would be the first dufus in town to fish out his swimming trunks. Maybe, just maybe, they had the teeniest little fear that Noah could be right. But they banded together, hunkered down and drowned in their chairs. I just wonder what went through their minds as they saw the heavens cry, the water rise and the ark begin to float.

Each time we gaze at the miracle of the rainbow, we know that God has made a covenant with man. There will never be another all-consuming flood. He told us in his Word and shows us with beautifully painted pastels gracefully arching across the sky.

No, we don't have to worry about water. Nor does a believer have to worry about hell. Christ paid that price for us. The only thing left for us to worry about is standing before him and seeing his face. Looking into his eyes and reading our lives. The total wipe-out of more tomorrows to right the wrongs. This is it. It is over. Life stands as it happened. It's history. And unlike modern-day historians, we cannot rewrite it. All the should-haves and could-haves won't change a thing. It's judgment day.

I don't know if you have ever read Daniel or Revelation. For an unbeliever, these books should be terrifying – they are scary enough for a believer. But they are also glorious and life-changing. They tell of the end of the world and the triumphant return of Jesus. I for one want to be that bride spoken of in Revelation, dressed in white linen waiting eagerly for my bridegroom to appear. I want the lamps of my home aglow – welcoming him as he rides up on his white charger. I don't want to ever again anticipate his return with fear and trembling and shame in my heart. I can honestly, from the bottom of my soul, tell you that I long for heaven. I am not afraid of death. On the contrary, I eagerly await it. Do you?

Time is running out.

Time is running out on the believer who has lived in the world, thinking that someday he or she will get back to God. Time is running out on the executive who traded God in for a country club membership. Time is running out on the college student who pledged a fraternity instead of pledging his life to God. Time is running out on the busy church worker who cheats on his income taxes.

Time is running out on the unbeliever who thinks he will someday make a commitment . . . just in case there is something to this story of Jesus. Time is running out and when it's gone, there will be no excuses. God has set in motion a plan and given us his blueprint so that we could make an intelligent decision. He tells us in his Word that his desire is that no one perish, but that everyone have life eternal. He gave us a great gift, free will. He doesn't impose himself on anyone but gives everyone the same information. It's up to us to examine his love letter and decide what to do with it. It's time to get serious and come to terms with your relationship to God.

He waited patiently for the men in the diner to come to their senses while Noah, the laughingstock of a cloud-free community, kept on building his ark. God waited 150 years. It's been almost 2,000 years, since Christ's death on the cross. And he's still waiting for his children to return to their Father. No one knows when our time will end, but the prophetic signs are rushing past us.

This is too important to casually believe your way is right without examining the evidence. For the unbeliever, it is the difference between heaven and hell. "For God so loved the world that he gave his one and only Son, that whoever believes in him shall not perish but have eternal life. For God did not send his Son into the world to condemn the world, but to save the world through him"[1]

For the Prodigal, it is the difference between standing before him in shame or hearing those glorious words, "Well done, thou good and faithful servant."[2]

I want to see a big-ol' smile spread crinkles around Jesus' eyes when he sees me coming. I want to run into his arms, jump in his lap and hug him for eternity. I want to ask him a million questions. I want to bow down before him and worship at his feet. I want to sing like an angel in a heavenly choir. I want to meet Daniel and become his best friend. There is so much to look forward to and we have an eternity to do it!

I want you to be excited about meeting your Savior and the Lord of your life. I don't want you to cringe like I used to do, hoping against hope for a cleft in the rock where you might hide at his second coming. I want you and I to be standing hand-in-hand looking toward heaven when the trumpet blows. I want to see the joy in your face when he says, "Well done, thou good and faithful servant."[3]

[1]John 3:16-17, NIV
[2]Matthew 25:21a, KJ
[3]Ibid

# ORDER FORM

**If you know someone who could be helped by reading this book check your local bookstores or order from us!**

Please send me _____ copies of **Potholes & Pigsties,**
**A Prodigal's Journey Home** @ $14.95 each =          $_____

Add Shipping & Handling:                              + $3.00

plus $1.24 per book sales tax (for Texas residents)  + $

Total Amount Enclosed (*check or money order*)        $_____


(*Please print*)

Name: _____

Address: _____

_____ Apt. # _____

City: _____

State: _____ Zip Code: _____


Send to:
**Pippin Publishing**
P. O. Box 8052
Waco, TX 76714-8052